# *In Sickness and In Wealth*

## Switched at Marriage, Episode 6

## Gina Robinson

Gina Robinson
SEATTLE, WASHINGTON

Book Layout ©2013 BookDesignTemplates.com
Cover Photos and Design by Jeff Robinson

In Sickness and In Wealth, Switched at Marriage 6/ Gina Robinson. — 1st ed.
ISBN 978-0692507667

## CHAPTER ONE

*Kayla*

Sticks and stones can break your bones, but pregnancy wands that read positive can absolutely ruin your life. And your phone conversations. Rule number one of stealth pregnancy test taking—never talk to the potential baby daddy while you're reading your results. *Never.*

I was staring at the dark, and I do mean blatant, second pink line on my pregnancy test wand. It was so deep pink, for a second I hoped I had double vision. Sadly, I didn't recall being bumped on the head recently. Though I did feel faint.

I cursed myself for not buying one of those tests that just tell you flat out "pregnant" in the little results window. Because even though I was clearly pregnant, my survival instincts had kicked in and I was in denial. Doubting the clear evidence before me.

For some odd reason, I found myself shaking the stick in the way you shake an old-fashioned thermometer to get the mercury down. As if I could shake away that second pink line and be done with it.

Don't you think pregnancy tests should be sold with more encouraging or sympathetic messages geared toward the test-taker? Like *congrats* with a zillion exclamation points for women who really want a baby. And another one that says, *Hugs, you'll figure it out* for those like me that really are only looking for peace of mind that they *aren't* pregnant.

And what about colorblind women? How do they even read the results? However, my results were so deeply pink that even Jus could probably see those thin pink lines of impending fatherhood. Otherwise known as the twins "doom" and "deep trouble."

"Kay? Kay, are you there? Have I lost you?"

Oh, yeah, I was still talking to Jus. Theoretically, anyway. In reality I couldn't breathe. My stomach seized up. I felt sick. And now my breasts suddenly ached in pregnancy sympathy.

I stared sideways at myself in the mirror. Were my breasts getting bigger? Was I looking fat? Did I have a faint baby bump already? The baby would be what, the size of a few cells? Maybe the tip of a pencil? I could be a real hypochondriac when the need arose.

"Yeah, I'm here." My voice shook, tremulous and thin as an old lady's.

If I retook this test in a few days, would that second pink line disappear? The test had to have a certain percentage failure rate, right? It couldn't be one hundred percent accurate. I dumped the instruction sheet out of the box, looking for hope in the form of statistics of just how incredibly unreliable these home test kits were.

I was skimming the fine print, Jus nearly forgotten, when the sound of his voice startled me back to reality.

"What's happened? Has something upset you?" His voice was deep with concern.

"What? No. What would have upset me?" My laugh was nervous. "Just suddenly got a frog in my throat." And a baby in my belly. Put there by you, buddy. I cleared my throat to make the point about the frog.

What was I going to do? I had a fake husband I was falling in love with and a scheduled divorce. Would Jus be a pretend daddy, too? If only the baby could be as fake as the marriage.

We'd been talking about Justin's mom and our trip to Italy. And how she wanted me to meet his brothers and dad.

The pregnancy test kit instructions—written in tiny, not easy to skim print—said the tests were inaccurate. Hah!

Oops! Only in the reverse of my situation. False negatives were much more common than false positives. If you got a negative result, but still believed you might be pregnant, retest in a few days. Your preggo hormones might not have fully kicked in enough to register yet.

If you got a positive and wanted a negative? You were out of luck, sister. You had pregnancy hormones galore floating through your system. They didn't just appear out of nowhere for no reason. A positive was pretty much as accurate as things got.

"Is this a bad time?" Jus was beginning to sound annoyed with me.

And to be honest, I was beginning to be angry with him. My current situation was all *his* fault. Him and his convincing story about needing the cover of not being a virgin to really sell this phony marriage had conned me into having sex with him in the first place. And look at the mess it had made.

Eric, for all his horniness, had never knocked me up. Jus probably had overachieving sperm, just like the rest of him. Why hadn't I thought of that before? Damn him! You'd think athletic guys would have the stronger sperm. But Justin's must have had some kind of superior intellect that foiled my birth control system. I'd taken my pills faithfully. What had happened? How had I fallen victim to their less than one percent failure rate with perfect use? I *would* win this kind of lottery. Just my stupid luck.

I had to soothe Jus and put him off guard until I could get over the initial shock and *think*. Just think. There had to be options. There were always options, even if I couldn't see them right now.

"As far as Naples, whatever Diana wants. I'm fine with anything." I couldn't make myself call his mother "Mom." Yet. Maybe I never would. I thought doing whatever she wanted would please him.

"Not *whatever* she wants." He laughed. "You obviously don't know Mom. She can be demanding. And overbearing. Never fear," he said in a knight-in-shining-armor voice. "I know how to handle her. I'll rein her in."

"Don't get cocky," I said, trying to sound like my normal self, though I was horribly distracted and having trouble concentrating on anything but that wand of motherhood before me. "Your mom has proven she can be incredibly wily."

Like popping in on us unexpectedly from halfway around the world. Crap, if she did that in Italy and inadvertently walked in on me in the middle of exhibiting a compromising pregnancy symptom, then what?

I was too distracted to properly concentrate on anything Jus was saying. Suddenly Italy seemed like a bad, bad idea. Was Diana one of those women with a knack for sniffing out pregnancy with the skill of a psychic? The pregnancy whisperer?

I made a mental note to avoid my own mom until I figured this out. She was so determined to have a grandchild, she'd been inspecting me for signs of giving her one since I first introduced Jus to her as my beloved hubs. She was so determined to imagine a pregnancy where there wasn't one, I shuddered at the thought of her getting hold of a genuine symptom.

I needed a strategy. I needed...a real husband. A partner I could actually confide my troubles in.

"Kay, are you *sure* you're all right? You sound like you're shaken up about something." There was that concern in his voice again.

Damn! I never did have a good poker face. Evidently I didn't have a good poker voice, either. "Sorry?"

He let out an exasperated sigh. As if I was hiding something from him. Which, of course, I was. He was a dangerous man. Too smart and intuitive. Funny how the two of us could hide things from the world, but I was already having trouble hiding this from him.

"Should I call back later?" He sounded tentative. As if he was just tossing the suggestion out there, hoping I would refuse.

"Yes!" I seized on the opportunity to escape before he changed his mind. Realizing too late I sounded way too eager and grateful for the suggestion.

"Sorry. I *am* distracted. So much to do before Italy!" I rattled off a list of meetings and tasks. "And I promised Sophia I'd bring Data by to play with her today. I really should go. Sophia will be expecting Data to be in one of her Doggy and Me outfits—"

"I miss you."

His words stopped me short as my heart tripped all over itself. If anything, I'd been expecting a rebuff. Another one of his admonitions not to girl up his dog.

I laughed, a nervous titter, really, because what else could I do? Was I going to be one of those emotional preggo girls, totally driven by hormones, who laughed and cried at all the inappropriate times? I felt like crying now. What was the correct response? An automatic *I miss you* wouldn't come off as genuine, even though it would have been.

I deflected. "I think you're missing sex."

I caught myself and laughed again, that same inane chirp. It was plaguing me like a nervous twitch and was just about as attractive. And then I ran on at the mouth, which was par for the course when I was anxious.

"Although we're not exclusive, are we? Don't we have one of those open fake marriages that are so popular now?" I didn't know why the thought of him with someone else irritated me so badly. Probably because now that I had a positive pregnancy test in front of me, I was getting irrationally possessive. "Now that I've initiated you—"

"I only want you." He paused.

And I thought, *This is as close to a declaration of love as I've gotten from him in private. If you love me, say it, Jus. Just say it. Because missing and loving aren't the same thing.*

"You've completely ruined me for any other woman." He hesitated again, getting my hopes up. "Kay, I don't want one of those open fake marriages."

Suddenly I had a lump in my throat. He could say the sweetest things at the oddest times. And still not go all the way. But maybe baby steps were safer, anyway. "Are you asking me to be exclusive?"

He laughed, almost a snort, as if he was laughing at himself. "Yeah. I've done it backwards. Marry you—"

"Well, not exactly marry. Fake a marriage."

"Semantics," he said. "You get the gist. Marriage and then ask you to go steady."

Tears formed in my eyes. Crappy pregnancy hormones. It was convenient now to blame everything on them. I laughed again and brushed the tears away with the back of my hand. "Jus, you're so old-fashioned. Go steady! What kind of crap is that?"

"Are you going to keep me in agony? Or is that a yes?"

I leaned back against the cool granite of the countertop and fought to swallow the lump. "Yes, that's a yes. And I miss you, too. And I *really* do have to run now."

"Me too." There was a huge smile in his voice. "Talk to you soon."

I turned around and stared at the pregnancy test again. A smart, cunning woman would destroy the evidence. I was smart, wasn't I? I grabbed it and wrapped it in a facial tissue. I was about to toss it in the wastebasket when I realized I couldn't throw it away in the penthouse. What if Magda, or the maid, found it in the trash?

I shuddered at the thought of them going through our garbage. Not that I thought they did. But one could never be too careful. I would have to take it outside and toss it in the garbage in the lobby or on the street.

I unwrapped it and stared at it again. If I threw the evidence away, would I convince myself I'd hallucinated the whole pregnancy? Probably. And this was one time I had to face reality.

I wrapped it up again and took it to the closet, where I hid it in one of my shoeboxes at the bottom of a stack. No one would ever find it there. I had so many shoes, sometimes I couldn't even find things in that pile of boxes.

I went back into the bedroom and collapsed on the bed. What was I going to do? Under ordinary circumstances, I'd call Britt. But she would only gloat and congratulate me for following her advice and hooking Jus for life. Since she didn't know my marriage was fake, she really wouldn't be any help.

I couldn't tell my parents, who would be ecstatic. I couldn't tell Jus. I shuddered at the thought. What was he going to think when I started waddling around? Would he still think I was hot? Would he revoke the recently agreed upon exclusivity clause?

My heart constricted. This wasn't how I wanted to catch Jus. I was startled at the thought. *Did* I want to catch Jus? When had I even begun considering it?

I made some quick mental calculations and looked at the calendar on my phone. This baby would just be a few weeks old when we divorced.

I took a deep breath and looked up the stats on miscarriages. It was an awful thought, but maybe I would spontaneously miscarry. It happened. Though only about ten to twenty percent of the time, according to my Google search.

One in ten wasn't such bad odds. Another article reported that doctors suspected that as many as fifty percent of pregnancies *may* end in miscarriage. But no one knew for sure. It was hard to authenticate or track because so many of them ended before the woman knew she was pregnant. Well, I knew. Did that mean I didn't still have that fifty percent chance?

I weighed my super-sucky options. As a "married" woman, I couldn't very well have the baby and give it up for adoption. Society frowned on that kind of thing unless I had a very good reason. And being filthy rich and married to one of Seattle's hottest nerds wasn't one of them.

I could terminate before anyone knew. But I would have to go through it all by myself. And keep it from everyone. I didn't think I could do it.

Or I could have it. And be connected to Jus, his family, and his *money, money, money* for the rest of my life. And, yes, that was what everyone would think, that I'd gotten pregnant as soon as possible in case Jus regretted his hasty, ill-conceived marriage. His quickie Reno wedding. And my reputation as a gold-digging, money-grubbing bitch would be sealed forever. So what? Let them think what they would. But I did care what Jus thought. If he thought the same, it would kill me.

Even so, why not just have the baby? Door number three was the option any sane, logical girl would take. Except...except I didn't want Jus for his money. I wanted a man who loved me madly. I wanted a great love, not a marriage of convenience. And more and more, I just wanted Jus. And was scared beyond reason that he wouldn't see this pregnancy in a positive light and as completely accidental as it really was.

Yes, he'd asked me to be exclusive. I *was* absolutely thrilled about that. And, as an aside, feeling supremely less guilty about kissing Lazer. Because that had definitely happened in our now defined pre-exclusive period.

I was also falling in love with Jus. But falling in love with someone and spending the rest of your life *tied* to someone and sharing custody, every other weekend and holidays, weren't the same thing.

I wanted him to want me. I wanted him to love me. Not because of any sense of obligation. Or because I was the mother of the heir to his billion-dollar Flashionista empire. I wanted him to fall in love with me. And I was running out of time. How could I balance all these plates of secrets I was suddenly spinning? Fool the world. Fool Jus. Maybe I was simply fooling myself.

Obviously, I couldn't keep the pregnancy a secret from him forever. There was a point when he would probably notice. Ha! But it was reasonable for a girl to wait to tell anyone until she was pretty sure the pregnancy would stick, right? And, okay, I was letting myself talk myself into things and deluding myself. That several-month deal was probably for back in the old days when you had to miss two or three periods and kill a rabbit before you could be certain you were pregnant. But what would it hurt to sit on this and see what happened before I, maybe unnecessarily, upset our delicate, budding relationship?

My phone buzzed in my hand. A text from Jus. A link to a YouTube video. When I clicked on it, it linked to Patrizio Buanne singing "*Luna Mezza Mare.*"

## CHAPTER TWO

*Justin*

I had a ridiculous smile on my face. The kind of smile a guy should have on his wedding day. The never-ending, brilliant beam of a groom as he stares at his bride at the altar and thinks, *How the hell did I get so lucky? How did I win that beautiful girl?*

Slowly, one small step at a time, I was conquering Kay's heart. Maybe more in the manner of a court jester than a dashing knight. But the style and means didn't matter. Only the end. It was like the old adage of boiling a frog—you turn up the heat so gradually, the frog doesn't realize it's being boiled until it's too late to jump out of the pot.

I was turning up the heat, the passion, and the emotion until it boiled over and Kay was mine. And damn if

I'd stop until I won. Kay was the girl for me. I was the guy for her. By the time our year together was up, she'd have no thought of leaving. We'd tear up that crazy postnup, laughing that we ever entertained the idea of divorcing. In the eyes of the law, from what it knew, in the eyes of everyone, we would be man and wife. Most importantly, in our own minds.

I was still mulling the legal crap, ramifications, and logistics over. We weren't genuinely married. And yet, for all the authorities knew, we were. We couldn't just slip into the courthouse and ask for a new marriage license. We could always renew our vows, but that wasn't the same thing as a new legal wedding, complete with license.

What about another country? I had every intention of making Italy special enough that Kay would be sentimental about it. Kay had always dreamed of a big, beautiful wedding. On our one-year, rather than divorcing, what if we "renewed" our vows in Italy, complete with an Italian marriage license? Or wherever she wanted to go. Flew friends and family in. Had one of those weddings billionaires are supposed to have.

Alone in my hotel room, I drummed my fingers on the dark wooden desk. Italy would be my coup de grace to any thought that we weren't really man and wife. I was going to win Kay's heart once and for all. Put all thoughts of any other guy, including Lazer, so far from her mind it would be like they'd never existed in the first place.

I was going to treat her like no other guy could. Spoil her. Make her laugh. Sing to her. Court her. And tell her I loved her.

I swallowed hard at the thought. *Tell her I love her.* Why was it so damn hard to do? If I blew it, there would still be ten more awkward months of marriage and rejection to go.

Kay didn't understand why I celebrated our weekly anniversaries for the first month, and now intended to celebrate our monthly ones, the mensiversary, if you were a stickler about terms. Every week was a victory, a step closer to the ID thief having no control over us. Two days before our two-month, sixty days would be over. Another milestone down. Another pile of digital video surveillance overwritten. My reputation and Flash that much safer. Just one more milestone after that.

Our little thieving ID stealer had been silent for almost a month. I should have been happy. I would have. If I'd seriously believed she'd given up. Fat chance of that. Too much money was at stake for her. Obviously someone who steals other people's identities and credit cards for a living would have to be greedy by nature. Pass up the gig of a lifetime? Why would she?

Dex and I had worked through several nights fine-tuning our software until it was a lean, mean recognition machine. It had generated a bunch of false positives. Women who looked kind of, sort of similar. But not her.

We needed more pictures, more data points. The software wasn't searching for a face the way a human would. It wasn't looking for a woman in a blond wig with red lipstick that looked a bit like Kay. It was looking for distinct facial characteristics that were unchangeable. At least without plastic surgery. Exactly how far apart the eyes were. How large they were. The exact shape. The length of the nose. The width of the mouth.

In some ways, it was better than a human. A human could be fooled by a dye job, a haircut or new style, or the tricks of makeup. But not our algorithms. The problem was, our little ID thief was camera shy. She didn't want to be caught. I might have been giving her too much credit, but she seemed to know enough not to turn full face to the camera.

We needed more facial data points, pure and simple. We needed a full-on facial shot so we could measure the metrics. In the meantime, our software turned up too many possible matches that went nowhere. Too many false leads. Too many girls who weren't the girl we were tracking. And even a few drag queens.

If I could draw a picture out of that bitch...

We tried to entice her out of hiding and into making a mistake. I spent too many evenings and afternoons hanging out in the bar in Reno during several "business" trips. I was going to Reno so often I was making the Reno site manager nervous.

In the hotel, I kept a high profile, hoping the con artist I'd shared a marriage ceremony with would approach me. I gambled and won enough cash to be a good mark. Let it spill out of my wallet, dangling as bait. Pretended to be drunk and susceptible again.

*Nothing.*

And then one evening, the photographer showed up. At least, I assumed it was him. It could have been someone either he or she paid to approach me.

I was having a beer at the bar after a long day at our distribution center when a guy in his thirties pulled up a stool next to me, too casually for it to have been accidental.

"Hey, aren't you that billionaire guy who owns Flashionista?"

I'd nodded, suddenly on alert.

"Your distribution center has brought a lot of good jobs to the area."

I studied him and nodded again. Did he think I needed my back patted?

"Got married recently, didn't you?" He was trying too hard to sound affable. "Saw something about it on the news." His eyes picked up an evil glint. "Saw something about another girl you were seeing on your wedding night. Quite the player."

He was either a douchebag or he wanted something. I turned away from him, heart racing. *Play it cool.*

"Seems like a guy in your position would pay a lot to get rid of any more pictures like the one I saw. Anything that would piss off the new wifey."

I took another sip of my beer, resisting the urge to knock him off his stool onto the beer-stained floor.

"Some other guy might." I fought to keep my tone even. "Not me. I don't have anything to hide. And even if I had, my wife is *exceptionally* understanding."

I'd been bullied too often to rise to his bait.

From the way he sat silently stewing, it was clear mine wasn't the answer he'd been expecting. I was on delicate ground. I wanted a lead, something that would give me a leg up on my adversary. But I couldn't give myself, or any weakness, away.

"Lucky guy," he said. "How about your investors and business partners?"

"They don't believe gossip," I said, evenly. "They believe me. Why shouldn't they? I always deliver on my promises."

I turned to look him in the eye. I couldn't resist giving him an unfriendly warning. "I don't take shit from anyone. And I don't fight fair."

It would have seemed like a non sequitur to an innocent guy. This guy took it at face value.

I had a bodyguard nearby. My PI had two guys running surveillance, hoping for something like this. I downed my beer and got up to leave. I was done with this douche. Let my team handle him.

As I walked out of the bar, my PI's guys followed Mr. Chatty. It was a dead end, again. For now. But Dex and I and my security team were getting everything we could on him. We'd break her operation and take her down. I just had to be patient.

The ID thief was playing things foolishly slowly. Didn't she realize that time was on *my* side? And I was about to strike.

My thoughts turned back to Kay. She'd seemed distracted and eager to get off the phone. I twisted my mouth to the side. I was worrying over nothing. Fake open marriages! Like I would tolerate that arrangement for long.

I smiled again at all the surprises I had in store for her in Italy. I was going to sweep her off her feet. Nothing was going to destroy this marriage. *Nothing*.

*Kayla*

Sophia was out of the hospital—temporarily, anyway. I'd promised her that when she got out, I would bring Data over to play with her. She was obsessed with dogs and puppies. Jus and I would have given her one, but caring for an animal on top of a sick child was more than Vicki could handle. After my call with Jus, I brushed Data and dressed her in a collar that matched my outfit, and headed south of town to Des Moines with Data to fulfill my promise.

Vicki and Sophia lived in an old, worn two-bedroom house so small it bordered on the new craze of tiny houses, sitting in the middle of a less than prosperous working-class neighborhood. It needed painting. And the lawn, like those of its neighbors, was brown from the recent heat spell. Most Seattleites didn't water. I felt guilty, and conspicuous, driving Justin's BMW, feeling the eyes of the neighbors on me.

I brought lunch for all of us, a picnic in the backyard, including special doggy treats for Data. Sophia had been watching for us through the window. If she'd been a normally healthy child, she would have bounded out to greet us. But her heart condition slowed her down, sapped her energy, and made her lethargic. She watched with eager eyes as Vicki answered the door and let us in.

Data warmed to her immediately. They were soon playing happily on the dry grass of the backyard while Vicki and I chatted and watched from the shade. The only saving grace of the place was the fenced backyard and the view of the very tops of the Olympic Mountains.

Data was as intuitive as her master. Even though she was still an energetic puppy, she played gently and patiently with Sophia, barking while she waited for her to catch up to her.

Vicki watched, protective and happy. "Look how happy she is! I would get her a dog, but..."

"If you ever decide you want one, Jus would gladly get her one." I took a sip of the bottle of lemonade I'd brought.

Vicki slid me a sideways glance and subtly raised one eyebrow. "You talk like the money is all his."

I laughed, nervous that I'd slipped up. I often forgot to regard Jus and I as "we." "Well, it is his. He earned it. I'm just on an allowance."

I sounded like a pampered princess. But I was actually an employee allowed petty cash, if you got right down to it. I had no claim on his money, other than what I was earning. But she couldn't know that. This was going wrong.

I changed the subject. "Sophia looks much better than when I last saw her in the hospital."

Vicki nodded. "Sometimes it's hard to believe, but she still needs a heart."

My heart broke a little for her. What could I offer her? Platitudes? Empty promises?

"I'm sorry. Jus and I both keep hoping for her." I paused. "It has to be hard raising her on your own."

I was selfishly thinking of my pregnancy. I wanted some words of encouragement from Vicki. Some advice. Some wisdom. Something to help me decide what to do. And, of course, I couldn't ask directly.

"Not so hard, because I love her." She stared at her daughter, with a half-smile playing at her lips and a look of absolute love shining in her eyes. "I wouldn't trade it away for anything."

I felt a stab of guilt.

She got a faraway look in her eyes. "I only have one regret—I never told her dad about her."

I tried not to let my surprise show. I guess it had been a natural assumption that the father had simply split and bailed on his responsibilities. "It's never too late, is it?"

Vicki took a deep breath. "He's dead. He died before I could tell him. Motorcycle crash."

"I'm sorry."

Her expression hardened. "Don't be. He wasn't the love of my life. He wasn't a great guy. He probably would have been a crappy dad. I wasn't going to stay with him. I just think it's too bad he died not knowing what a great kid he was going to have. That he was leaving a legacy behind."

She sighed. "If he'd known, he may have deserted her, us. He probably would have, knowing him. He wasn't the type to be tied down. But he had a right to know and make his own choice."

Vicki sure knew how to unintentionally twist the stiletto.

I felt suddenly cold and clammy, nauseated.

Vicki looked at me with concern. "You're pale. Are you okay?"

I forced a smile and lied. "I'm fine. Just, you know, that time of the month when the hormones go crazy and throw my internal thermostat off."

She smiled at me. "I know that feeling. Sucks being a girl sometimes."

Sophia laughed as Data licked her face. Vicki's smile became full-blown sunshine. "And sometimes it's the best thing ever. Wait until you have kids."

Oh, yeah. I couldn't wait.

"Look, Mommy, look!" Sophia tossed a small ball for Data to fetch.

Vicki clapped and waved to her and turned to me. "When will Justin be back?"

"Next week. Just in time for us to fly to Italy together." Italy. I was suddenly dreading it. Maybe Vicki was right. Jus had a right to know he was going to be a daddy.

I tried to picture telling him. Tried to imagine his reaction. I glanced at Sophia. Jus loved children. And had a knack with them. But was he ready for one of his own?

A cold fear crept over me. *He loves kids.* How much? Enough to take one away from me when we divorced? He had the money and resources. Way more than I did.

Deep down I knew I would never abandon my baby. I loved children, too, and had always dreamed of having them.

But not like this. More like when I had real husband, a satisfying career, and was living in my own house. When it was planned and I was ready. When life was more settled.

I certainly never imagined having one with Jus. With Jus. Could I really leave the father of my baby? I felt suddenly suffocated and trapped. And at the same time, excited at the thought of staying with Jus.

I should tell him. But this wasn't your ordinary situation. He could toss me out. Say I'd broken the terms of our agreement. I couldn't remember if there was a clause in the postnup for an accidental pregnancy. Probably not, given the no-sex-expected clause I'd insisted on.

I would tell him. Eventually. *If* it became absolutely necessary. In the meantime, I had to make up my mind about him. Was I enough in love with him to make a real life with him? Did I want to be his wife, his *real* wife?

If I did, I had to make him fall in love with me.

# CHAPTER THREE

*Justin*

I flew from Reno to Columbus, Ohio. To the second of our three distribution centers. The third was in New Jersey. Columbus and Reno were the distribution center capitals of the country. Row after row of warehouses of brand-name stores side by side. It didn't matter whether we were talking upscale brand or lowbrow, all the warehouses looked the same, distinguished only by the logos of their signs.

Originally, I was supposed to fly home to Seattle and then to Milano with Kay. A problem with one of our fulfillment processes kept me in Columbus longer than I intended. I called Ophie and had her arrange for Kay to fly out of Seattle on a hired business jet and pick me up in Columbus. From there we'd fly to Milano.

The schedule wasn't ideal. A red-eye flight from Seattle. The jet landed in Columbus at almost three in the morning. Which didn't matter to me. I was used to all-nighters and living on too little sleep. To me, the concept of time had become flimsy. I traveled so often I didn't get attached to any one time zone. It was enough when I was home in Seattle to settle back into Pacific Time. The first few years of Flash I hardly slept at all. If I'd been a normal twenty-one-year-old I would be partying all night in college and pulling all-nighters studying for exams anyway. This was no hardship.

As my driver pulled up alongside the sleek jet, my pulse quickened at the thought of seeing Kay for the first time in weeks. I could almost smell her. Taste her kiss on my lips. Missing someone when you're away from them was supposed to be a sure sign of true love. If true, I had it bad. I'd missed Kay the moment I stepped away from her. The only thing that had changed since college was the intensity.

Obsession was not the right word for my feelings. Kay had always been the one girl who saw past the geek, now past the money, to the guy I was. How could a billionaire like me ever know whether a girl wanted *him*, or simply what his money could buy?

Since being with Kay, since talking her into this marriage, or whatever it was, arrangement, I thought of her every minute I couldn't be with her. I hungered and thirsted for her. Unquenchable. Missing her laugh and her smile. The camaraderie. The intimacy of her, and only her, being in on my deepest secret.

No matter how much time we spent together, I was never sated. I wanted more. So much more.

Having a crew onboard meant more acting and playing the part of happy newlyweds. The lines continually blurred, becoming more indistinct every day. Like actors who fell in love with their costars, it would have been so easy to believe this script was real. With no final act where we divorced.

The flight attendant, Merry, welcomed me onboard and introduced me to the pilot, who waved and returned to preparing for a quick turnaround and takeoff. Merry offered me refreshments while my bags were loaded and the plane prepared for our transatlantic flight. I looked around for Kay, my heart in my throat. My desire pulsing. It must have been too damned obvious.

Merry took pity on me. "Mrs. Green retired shortly after takeoff from Seattle, sir. I believe she's waiting for you in the bedroom."

Poor Merry. She'd tried to say it with a professional, straight face. But a hint of a smile played at the edges of her lips, like she knew what she was saying was full of innuendo and promise.

Kay waiting for me in the fine silk sheets, dressed in a whisper of sexy lingerie. My pulse roared.

I nodded and tried not to look as eager and horny as I was. I practically ran to the bedroom as the plane taxied down the runway. By the time I pulled the bedroom door open, we were airborne. And I was flying high with the thought of Kay.

A light was on on the nightstand. Kay was in bed—sound asleep, her blond hair tumbling over her pillow. She wore evening makeup, the kind I'd told her turned me on. Long false lashes. Sultry, smoky eyes. Red lipstick in a shade so deep I could actually tell it was red. She was tucked beneath the covers with one slender arm exposed, the strap from her lingerie in my favorite shade of blue sliding off her shoulder.

I clenched my fists and took a deep breath. I wanted to dive into that bed and into Kay and lose myself. I stripped off my jacket and tossed it over a chair. Pulled my shirt free of my slacks. Kicked off my shoes. Sat on the edge of the bed. Brushed her hair out of her eyes. Traced her arm with my fingers.

She didn't even stir.

"Kay?" I whispered, gently shaking her.

Still no movement.

I slid out of my clothes and into bed. Damn, she was wearing a negligee designed to give me a hard-on for life. I curled up behind her and pressed into her, breathing into her ear. "Kay, baby."

Nothing but the soft, even rhythm of her breathing. She was practically comatose. Unless I wanted to make love to an unconscious woman, I wasn't getting lucky tonight.

*Kayla*

I woke to the gentle whir of airplane engines. The sky was still dark outside the jet windows toward the rear of the plane. I'd become so used to the lights of the city sparkling into the penthouse, I'd left the shutters open. That's what homey was becoming to me, being on display and feeling like I was sleeping in the middle of the open sky. We were driving into a hint of dawn over the nose of the plane. Next to me, the guest pillow was rumpled and smelled like Jus.

*Jus!*

I sat up and looked around. The bed was empty. So was the room. His jacket was slung over a chair.

So much for being a seductress. I'd meant to wait up for him. Give him a greeting that would make him happy. Instead, I'd zonked out completely, fallen asleep in full makeup. There were lipstick and foundation stains on my pillowcase. And I was sure I looked lovely with my tangled hair, smeared makeup, and one false eyelash coming off. Why hadn't he woken me?

I slid out of bed and took a quick shower, hoping he'd join me. Airplane shower sex had to be on his list, right?

He left me alone and disappointed in the shower. I dressed and made myself presentable. I found him in the main body of the airplane, sitting in a plush leather seat, working on his laptop at a table. Working, always working.

His back was to me. I slipped behind and beside him and slid my arms around his neck. "Welcome back. Why didn't you wake me?"

He looked up and gave me a sweet, quick kiss that made me ache inside with want, and what, if it wasn't love budding, was a damn good imitation.

His lips curved in a smile. "I tried." He stroked my cheek. "But waking you was like trying to wake the dead. I figured you needed your sleep and gave up."

Did he sound disappointed? Selfishly, I hoped he was. *I* was. Suddenly I was becoming the sex fiend in this relationship, craving his eager, caring touch.

"Sorry." I put on a playful pout to show him I genuinely was. "I took something for motion sickness. It was supposed to be non-drowsy. But it must have knocked me out."

I was lying. During the last week I'd become hormonally tired. I'd been in denial before, but now I'd been assailed by the first damning symptom of pregnancy—bone-weary exhaustion and a desperate need for sleep at the drop of a hat. But it wouldn't do to make him suspicious right out of the gate. Not that he would be looking for signs of pregnancy. But why court trouble?

He frowned. "Was there turbulence?"

I shook my head. "Just the fear of it."

"Statistically, flying is the safest mode of transportation—"

"I suppose you've heard the one about the statistician who drowned in a river that averaged three feet deep?"

He laughed. "The fear is all in your head. You have to face it."

"I did. With the help of over-the-counter meds."

He shook his head. "We have a big day ahead of us. Are you ready for Milan?" He snapped his laptop shut a little too casually.

Jus was always understanding and kind. Eric would have been in a rant or a major man pout over a missed opportunity. Reunion sex was sacred to him.

"I've been ready for Milan my whole life." I slipped into the chair across from Jus. "I'm hungry." The sudden sick hunger was another symptom I was just discovering. "What time is it? Time for breakfast yet?"

"It's time for breakfast somewhere in the world. If you're hungry, we'll eat." He signaled for Merry.

What I was really hungry for was him. Why didn't I just tell him? Because of the baby. Because I had to be sure. About everything.

*Justin*

*Via Monte Napoleone* was the most important street in the *Quadrilatero della moda,* the fashion district of Milan. Every major Italian designer, every major designer period, had a boutique along the brick streets. As a surprise for Kay, I'd booked private appointments at half a dozen of her favorites. I'd asked Sarah for help choosing which designers. And asked her to use her contacts. She was our Italian buyer. She knew the fashion industry, and Kay's tastes, much better than I did. At heart, I was a programmer, a guy who thought baggy jeans and T-shirts were all the style I needed, and who still confused colors and couldn't tell pink from gray. Sometimes I was still surprised to be in the business I was. It was all Riggins' fault.

I sat in the perfumed private dressing room area, beneath a crystal chandelier, in a chair reserved for guests of the shopper—husbands, benefactors, friends—sipping a fine Italian wine. I was surrounded by mirrors that flattered the shopper, and lighting designed to make anyone with money enough to be there look good.

I'd insisted Kay try on sexy, formfitting outfits. Everything should show off her fabulous figure. If I was going to have a trophy wife, she should look it. She always looked hot. But I wanted the very best in Italian fashion for her.

Italian women, especially the Milanese, knew how to dress to provoke the male eye to ardor and lust. It was a special pride of theirs. The women were thin, yet lush, in their tight clothes and stiletto shoes. They caught the eye with their sultry looks. Kay was blond, but she could have been one of them, their American sister.

She came out of the dressing room in a violet dress as tight as second skin and a pair of four-inch heels. My mouth went dry. My pulse raced. All I could think about was sex.

"Get it." My voice nearly cracked. I was that desperate and horny.

She turned sideways, biting her lip as she studied her reflection. Her hand skimmed her perfectly flat stomach. She frowned, looking unhappy and displeased with what she saw. Kay had abs ordinary girls would kill for. I cursed the sorority for instilling a sense of unrealistic body perfection. She looked pretty damn perfect to me.

"I don't know—"

"Get it," I reiterated.

She smiled uncertainly at me. "You're spoiling me. It's expensive—"

Another girl would have taken advantage of my generosity and abused it. Kay had to be convinced. Which was one reason I loved her. She didn't take my generosity for granted. "What's money for if you can't spend it on the woman you love?"

Too much? Maybe. Angelina, the Italian woman helping us, smiled at the *amore*.

"I love that violet color. It looks great on you and matches your eyes," I said, trying to encourage Kay.

Her forehead creased before she broke into a soft laugh. "Jus! This dress is blue. And so are my eyes, and you know it. I'm not Elizabeth Taylor with her famed violet eyes."

I shrugged. "You are to me."

It hadn't escaped my notice that she'd begun wearing my favorite colors. I was enormously pleased.

She turned to Angelina. "He's colorblind."

Angelina made a sympathetic noise.

"Don't you ever wish you saw the world as it really is?" Kay asked me.

"No. I like my version of it just fine." I motioned to Angelina. "We'll take it. Mail it home with the rest."

*Kayla*

Angelina spoke perfect English. Inside the dressing room, I held my breath as she unzipped the back of the dress for me. I couldn't have gotten in and out of it without her help. The dress, all the clothes Jus had bought me, were beautiful, the kinds of things you see in high-fashion magazines and dream about. But don't think you'll ever be able to afford.

Ordinarily, I would have been on top of the world, waiting for fall when the season turned so I could wear these new luxuries. But given my current condition, it seemed a waste to buy a dress for fall unless it was maternity fashion.

As I stepped out of it, I turned to Angelina. "Can this dress be taken out?"

She gave me a curious look. "You're so slender, *signora*. It's a perfect fit. You don't need it let out at all."

I leaned into her and put a hand on her arm, glancing cautiously toward the door as if Jus could hear. I lowered my voice. "I'm pregnant." I put a finger to my lips. "My husband doesn't know."

So the first person I told was a saleswoman, a complete stranger, who couldn't have cared less, except that I might balk at more purchases and cut her commission. Even so, I felt lighter at sharing with someone.

She nodded knowingly. "I can keep the secret. Congratulations."

I pinched my mouth to one side. "Hmmmm...thanks."

She sensed my worry. "You aren't happy?"

I couldn't say too much. "I'm uncertain. This wasn't planned. We've only been married a few months." I paused. I was running off at the mouth. "Can you show me anything that will hide a pregnancy for a few months longer?"

She nodded. "Of course. But you won't be able to hide it in the bedroom." Italians were frank about sex.

"No, of course not. He'll have to know soon. But as for the rest of the world, I'd just as soon keep them in the dark as long as possible."

Angelina studied my figure. "Your husband wants to show you off. We'll have to be very clever to get what we want past him. Something with ruching, I think."

I nodded, relieved.

"Have you been to the *Duomo di Milano* yet?"

It seemed and odd, out-of-the-blue question, especially from a saleswoman.

"Not yet. We haven't had time for sightseeing," I said. "We will before we leave Milan."

"It's very beautiful. One of the largest cathedrals in Europe. Light a candle and ask Saint Gerard Majella to watch over you while you're there. He's the patron saint of pregnant women. You'll want his help."

Yes, but did you ask saints of pregnancy to help you lose a pregnancy? A miscarriage would solve so many problems.

*Justin*

I wanted to buy Kay everything, including the world. A good portion of the clothes in it, anyway. I expected her to be thrilled with the adventure of buying a completely new fall wardrobe in one of the fashion capitals of the world. At the most exclusive boutiques. With personal attention and all the privilege of money. If money couldn't buy me love, I was damn well going to use it to bribe some affection from Kay.

And turn her into the hottest piece of eye candy in Seattle.

To my surprise, she fought me on the clothes—dresses, skirts, jeans, and blouses in fabrics so soft they were unbelievable. When she eased off and relented even slightly, she tried to sneak flowing, blousy, loose-fitting clothes past me. What the hell? Suddenly she was fiscally conservative? And modest about her body? Where was that partying sorority girl I knew and lusted after in college?

I appreciated her concern for my wallet. She was sensitive about looking like a gold digger. But damn, it made me all too aware that she wasn't my wife, but my employee. And these days, this was mere pocket change to me.

*Make me happy. Behave like a real wife and buy the damn clothes, Kay. Run me broke. Give me a chance to bitch with the guys about how much my old lady spends on rags. Give me that fantasy.*

And then she saw a "sweet little pair of shoes" in the window of Gucci. Girly squeal! And that was all she wrote. Her mood lightened and the old Kay I knew emerged, laughing and joyous as she bought pair after pair of stilettos, pumps, and platforms. Every brand, from Gucci to Jimmy Choo. She didn't constrain herself to Italian brands. Shoes that gave her a good four to six inches of height and made me think about nothing but sex. Like an addict, she lost all restraint as she moved on to necklaces, gloves, jewelry, and purses.

There was nothing like Italian leather for purses. And nothing like Italian gold for jewelry.

"Only eighteen karat and above for the Italians!" she said with a glint in her eyes. "Look for the 750 mark and we're golden."

I rolled my eyes at her bad pun, happy to see her so happy. Elated to see my plan working. "That was bad, Kay. So bad."

She only kissed me and laughed.

Damiani, Bulgari, and Milan's own Buccellati. We bought it all.

We spent nearly five days in Milan, shopping and meeting with prospective suppliers, budding designers hungry to be showcased on Flashionista and make their name. Kay knew how to handle and flatter them. She modeled their clothes for me.

We ate fabulous Italian food, though Kay tended to pick at hers. And drank no more than a glass of wine a day. "If I eat like the Italians, I'll never fit into my new clothes! How do the Italian women stay so thin?"

At night, she wore the jewelry and the shoes she insisted she had to have now and we fucked like honeymooners. She wanted it hard. Hard. *Harder, Jus!*

There was no tenderness in it, just passion and abandon. And lust. Plenty of raw lust.

On our last day in Milan, I took her to the big white Gothic Cathedral of Milan, designed by Leonardo da Vinci. The outside was magnificent. Kay insisted on going in. The inside was disappointing compared to the exterior. Dark and damp. There were better, more majestic Italian cathedrals to see.

I caught Kay buying a candle to light. I laughed at her. "What are you praying for? More money? More good fortune?"

She laughed softly and covered my mouth. "Shhh! You can't be irreverent here. We're in a church!" She shook her head. "Obviously, you have no clue about my character."

"I don't?" I stared at her, waiting for her to continue. "Enlighten me? What are you going to pray for? World peace?"

She shook her head. "You are so rotten. Stop with the beauty pageant crap. If you must know, I was going to pray for something more personal."

I waited for her.

"I'm going to light a candle to one of the patron saints of marriage. Living with you, I need all the help I can get." She winked, teasing me in that flirtatious way that made my heart race. "Maybe Saint Priscilla, the Patron Saint of Good Marriages." She took my hand and batted her eyes at me. "So you'll keep buying me everything I want." Her eyes danced. "You do want a *good* marriage, don't you, baby?"

I swallowed hard, resisting the urge to say I wanted a *long* marriage. I wanted her for life. *She* wanted a good marriage? Was she just toying with me? Because she already had me dancing on her string. "Good is good."

"That was totally eloquent." She leaned her head against my arm and smiled up at me adoringly. "Or maybe Saint Rita of Cascia, Saint of Difficult Marriages." She put on a pout. "You drive me crazy at times. Like now."

She was wearing a pair of Gucci shoes we'd bought the first day in Milan. They made her nearly even with me in height. She whispered in my ear, "No one who knew the truth would say we don't have a challenging marriage, Jus."

She grinned. "Though not in the usual way." She bit her lip. "Or maybe to Saint Valentine, the Patron Saint of Happy Marriages. What do you think? Good marriage? Happy marriage? Difficult marriage? Whom do we appeal to?"

My heart hammered. "I didn't think you were religious. And you're not Catholic."

"No, but when in Rome. One of the saleswomen who helped me the first day suggested I light a candle here while we're here. She saw how happy we were and said lighting a candle was insurance to help our marriage stay happy. What can it hurt?" Her smile was dazzling.

My heart was in her hands. Did she know how much I wanted what she was teasing about so lightly? I shrugged. "Or when in Milan."

I pulled a handful of bills from my wallet and handed them to her. "I'm partial to Saint Valentine. But why shouldn't we have everything? Good and happy, and definitely not difficult. Light a candle to each of them."

# CHAPTER FOUR

*Kayla*

Compared to Milan, Naples was meh. But then, what wasn't? Naples was dirty and old. A large city. Filled with history, yes. But after the heady shopping in Milan? Just about anything would have been a disappointment.

Because it was my first trip to Italy, it was easy to forget that Jus had been dozens of times. Nearly every summer since he was little. His parents had had the rugby tournament business forever. Jus spoke Italian fluently. It shouldn't have surprised me. I loved listening to the romantic language fall off his tongue, making that deep voice of his even sexier.

I didn't speak a word beyond *pizza, ciao,* and *gelato.* But after being in the country a few days, I was beginning to pick up the cadence of the language. In Naples, the sound of the language was different.

"They speak *Napolitano* here," Jus told me while we arrived. "It's a different dialect from official Italian. Naples used to be its own duchy until the regions of Northern Italy consolidated the country and forced their language on it."

We were in a hired car taking us to the campus where the tournament was being held. Jus sat next to me, squeezing my hand in the air-conditioned car. Outside, the heat radiated in waves off the pavement.

I was nervous about this meeting. But maybe I could pawn my growing morning sickness off on mere nerves. It was nearly August. A few more days and all of Italy would shut down for the summer. It was hot, as Southern Italy was bound to be in the prime of summer. Naples was on the water. I imagined the beaches—were there beaches in Naples?—would be crowded.

Justin's insecurities had begun to spring. We'd come directly from meetings with a buyer in Milan. I'd offered up the suggestion to change into something more comfortable before we flew to Naples. He said there wasn't time, and suggested the summer dress I'd worn to our meetings was perfectly appropriate. For what was essentially a collegiate rugby camp? I wasn't so sure. But I found myself dressed in a tight sundress and heels, dripping in Italian gold necklaces and baubles, wearing a pair of Gucci sunglasses. And feeling pretentious. But there you had it. Jus was the baby. He had something to prove to the older boys.

We wound through the city. I'd been so preoccupied with my problems, I'd left all the planning of our trip to Jus. I hadn't even bothered to look ahead to where the rugby tournament was being held.

"At a local college," Jus said, and rattled off an Italian name. "They hold it here every year. We'll be staying at a nearby *pensione*. It's not fancy. More like a dorm." He frowned.

I got the feeling he wasn't filled with warm fuzzies at the memories here.

He smiled at me. "We just have to endure these next few days and then the fun begins. You'll love the Amalfi Coast." He squeezed my hand as we pulled down a tree-lined street and came to a stop in front of an ancient-looking building. "With any luck we can escape Naples for a day and take in Vesuvius and Pompeii."

Everything in Italy was full of history.

Jus pulled his hand free and sent a text. A minute later, Diana Green appeared on the front steps of the *pensione* along with two big, hot guys who bore a resemblance to Jus.

Jus turned to me. "Brace yourself. You've entered the sports zone. Nothing but rugby talk for days on end." He made a point of shuddering before he handed me out of the car.

Diana rushed up first to greet us. She was dressed as you might imagine—in sports gear emblazoned with the logo of their company, Rugby Explorers. She was more tanned than the last time I'd seen her. Toned and tall. She hugged her son and then me. She pulled back to arm's length and studied me.

My heart stopped. For some reason I was convinced she would see I was pregnant right then. As if she had some great pregnancy-detecting superpower.

Her critical eye glided over me. "You look very Milanese today. Are those Gucci sunglasses?" She raised one eyebrow.

Jus pulled me free from her. "We came straight from business meetings in the fashion district—"

He was cut off from finishing his sentence, ambushed by his brothers. Grabbed and wrestled around, hugged, teased. His brothers were each six foot five, at least. They dwarfed poor Jus, who was over six foot.

"Boys! Let your baby brother go." Diana called a truce, but her smile was one of pure delight. As if boys will be boys and the horseplay was part of the fun. She made the introductions.

Jus bristled at being called a baby.

And now I could see exactly what Diana had meant when I first met her. Jerod and Jeremy were exactly the kind of guys I used to go for. Confident and charmingly cocky in the way strong athletes are. In full control of their bodies. Graceful in a masculine sense. Alpha dogs.

Jus was the runt of her litter of boys. Muscular, but slightly built compared to the other two. And four or five inches shorter. You could not have gotten his two brothers in skinny jeans like Jus wore, for example. Their thighs were roughly twice the size of one of Justin's, and would look ridiculous encased in tight denim. Their biceps bulged beneath black T-shirts. Just the fact that they were wearing black in the heat made them badass, even though it seemed to be one of Rugby Explorers' signature colors.

Called out by their mother, the big Js left Jus alone. And fuming. Suddenly they were all charm. The questions and compliments flew.

"Jus, you married above yourself." Jerod winked at me as he grabbed my bags and carried them inside. "Surprised the hell out of us. We never thought you'd marry at all. What girl would want you? Kayla, what does a beautiful girl like you see in a dweeb like our baby bro?" His voice had just a hint of an Italian accent.

"He's just so darn adorable!" I smiled at Jus, who, had he been a cartoon, would have had steam coming out of his ears.

Jus took my hand and flashed me a smile of gratitude. "Some women just have good taste. Where's Dad?"

"Kirk had tourney business to take care of." Diana followed us in. "He'll join us for dinner."

Inside, the *pensione* was pleasant, but plain. As Diana showed us to our room, four or five college-age guys burst down the hall, loud and boisterous, big and muscled, like football players. Typical rugby builds. They gave me the up and down as they brushed past us. One paused enough to flash me a flirtatious smile.

Diana gave them a cheery wave. "Take it easy tonight, boys. The tourney starts bright and early tomorrow morning."

She was such a mom. To everyone, it seemed. And it was clear she adored boys. She'd probably been a tomboy herself.

She returned her focus to us. "Dinner's at eight. Justin, you're going to love this. In your honor, we're eating at your favorite seafood place tonight!" She beamed at him.

Jus clearly wasn't used to being the main attraction and being spoiled. He grinned. "Paolo's?"

She nodded.

"It's been a few years," Jus said. "He still running the place? I thought he was going to retire and turn it over to his son."

Diana laughed. "Like that is *ever* going to happen. Paolo can't stand being idle. Or letting anyone else run his kitchen.

"He hasn't forgotten how you fixed his computer and built his website last time he saw you. 'Your boy saved a my business!'" She made an Italian hand gesture I didn't understand, but was obviously supposed to be mimicking Paolo's joy.

"He's got a fresh catch of *polpetto* he's saving just for you!" She opened the door to a room. "You have an en suite bath if you want to freshen up beforehand."

I stifled a yawn. I needed a nap. My bedtime was becoming embarrassingly early.

"Tired?" Diana asked me with that searching look again.

Last time I'd seen her, she'd warmed up to me. Her manner was friendly now. But she was obviously wary and totally wrapped up in the pleasure of having all her boys around her. Protective of Jus. I hoped she also wasn't as observant and intuitive. Jus had to get his traits from somewhere.

"Jet-lagged." I smiled at her.

"But you've been here, what, four or five days already?" Diana said gently.

I forced myself to keep smiling. "I'm not much of a traveler. I can't seem to shake it." *Or the grandchild I'm carrying for you.*

She put a gentle hand on my arm. "Take a nap. You'll want to be fully awake for dinner so you can enjoy the feast Paolo's making special for us. Have you ever seen the movie *Big Night*?"

I shook my head.

"Too bad. If you had, you'd know what I mean. He's preparing us his signature dish along with the rest of the feast." She turned to her son. "Justin can catch up with his brothers and me while you rest."

The last thing I remembered was lying down "just for a few minutes." I didn't wake up until several hours later when Jus gently shook me.

"Hey, sleepyhead. Time to get ready for dinner." His voice was gentle, but concerned. "You slept a long time. You aren't sick, are you?"

I rubbed my eyes and glanced at the clock on the wall. Crap! I had to hurry if we were going to make it to dinner on time. I'd slept so long I had bedhead. Was I drooling, too? "I'm fine." I sat up and rubbed my eyes.

"It's taking you a while to adjust to the time difference." There was that worry in his voice again.

I shrugged it off.

He sighed. "Next time we'll make sure to get you remedies to prevent jet lag."

Paolo's was only a few blocks away from the *pensione*. From the outside it was a candidate for the Italian version of *Diners, Drive-Ins and Dives*. Inside, it wasn't much fancier. But it smelled delicious, like everything Italian. Since most of the Italians in America immigrated from the south of Italy, our version of Italian food is southern in nature. In that way, Paolo's smelled homey, yet old world and exotic at the same time. Like the very best, high-end Italian food in the States. It definitely wasn't chain restaurant fare.

Justin's dad was waiting for us. It wasn't hard to spot him. Justin's two older brothers were younger copies of him. Jus looked more like his mom. Even down to her build. She was tall for a woman, but not as big-boned as he was in proportion to her size.

Kirk was a big former jock who looked like he'd played football at some point during his younger days. He had that air about him. Friendly. With a deep voice that was an older, more gravelly version of Justin's. At least Jus had inherited that much.

Kirk greeted me with a crushing hug. Gave his immediate blessing to our union. And told me to call him whatever I wanted. "Kirk. Dad. Hey you. Doesn't matter to me. Don't want you to feel awkward when you're trying to get my attention. Getting used to calling your in-laws by some name, any name, takes time. When Diana and I first got married, I spent a good three months avoiding using any name at all for her dad. Damn inconvenient."

I smiled, liking him on sight. He was big, but sweet like Jus in the way he was trying to put me at ease.

Paolo scurried out of the kitchen and greeted us each, including me, in the Italian fashion, with an air kiss on each cheek. He smiled at me, used so many Italian hand gestures he may as well have been speaking sign language, and rattled off a string of rapid-fire Italian I had no hope of understanding.

Jus seemed to follow it. Soon the two of them were involved in an animated discussion. Jus was even using his hands to talk, too. Which was so sexy it was crazy. All the Greens were soon in on it, laughing and interjecting. Gesturing. Finally, Paolo slapped Jus on the back and we took our seats at a prime table.

I was seated next to Jus, with Kirk on the other side of me. Diana and the others across from me. The wine immediately began to flow.

Jeremy quickly noticed I wasn't keeping up with the others and drinking my share. "You have a non-drinker on your hands, Justin."

I shook my head. "Hardly. I was in the hardest-partying sorority at my school. But too much wine makes me sleepy. My jet lag doesn't need any help, thank you very much. Besides, I'm half your size." I winked at him like I admired his big manliness.

Jerod laughed and refilled my glass. "I'll buy you some NoDoz."

I liked his brothers and the boisterous atmosphere of his family. Jeremy and Jerod were exactly the kind of guys I enjoyed hanging with. I could flip them as much crap as I wanted and they deflected and flipped it back.

"Do you play rugby?" Jerod asked as we devoured a plate of antipasti.

I shook my head. "I knew a few girls in college who were on our college team. That's the extent of my knowledge of the game. Women's rugby is gaining in popularity in the States. Maybe it will eventually replace soccer as the club sport of choice."

"You've *never* played?" Jeremy looked astounded, almost as if I'd committed some kind of heresy.

"No." My stomach started to feel funny. And the smells that had been delicious a few minutes ago took on a sour edge.

"Not even once?" Kirk passed me a loaf of bread.

I gratefully took it and tore off a chunk. The Italians put the bread in the middle of the table. You grabbed or tore off what you wanted. They didn't stand on ceremony. Like slicing bread.

"Not even once." The bread went down well.

Jerod poured himself another glass of wine. "We'll have to get you out on the field. You can't be a Green without playing rugby."

"What do you mean? Justin can." Jeremy laughed.

"He's a special snowflake." Jerod nudged Jus beneath the table while Jus glared. "Delicate constitution, right, Jus? Poor baby bro. Might get hurt."

Jus glared at him.

"Lighten up on the baby, Jer. He keeps a mean score sheet." Jerod laughed.

"Boys." Kirk used the dad voice. "Your brother isn't brawny, but he's got game smarts. He can out-coach either of you." He winked at his youngest son. "By the way, I need you to fill in for me and take my team tomorrow afternoon. I have a business meeting with the university I can't get out of."

"Sure, Dad." Jus didn't look thrilled at the idea.

"Do you like sports, Kayla?" Jerod leaned across the table, penetrating in the way he waited for my answer. Looking roguishly hot.

"I'm into men who play them." The flirt came out accidentally.

Diana shot me a sharp look.

Next to me, Jus set his jaw.

"And especially into guys who coach them." I grabbed Justin's arm and gave him an adoring look.

His face lit up. A busboy cleared the antipasti and plates. Two of Paolo's staff came out of the kitchen, carrying trays of steaming soup.

Kirk rubbed his hands together. "And here it is! The main event. You're in for a treat, Kayla. No one makes *zuppa di pesce* like Paolo! It's his specialty. People come from all over Naples for it."

As a bowl was set in front of me, my stomach grumbled. A gag rose in my throat. *Crap.* I swallowed hard against the bile rising in my esophagus. Morning sickness *would* choose now, a most inconvenient time, to make its first appearance.

I got my first glimpse of my bowl of soup—clams steamed open in their shells, tiny whole fish with their eyes staring accusingly back at me, whole shrimp, still in their shells, complete with legs, long antennae, and beady eyes, and whole baby octopi swimming in a tomato base. It was like a trip to the zombie aquarium in my bowl.

My stomach roiled. Didn't the Italians know you're supposed to clean the fish before you cook it? And devein the shrimp and take them out of their shells? And who eats baby octopus?

I didn't want to be close to the earthy nature of my food. I wanted my food the American way—clean and sanitized to the point where you'd never imagine your meat actually came from a real animal.

Just then Kirk took a spoonful of baby octopus and ate it whole, chewing rigorously.

I tried not to wince as I imagined what was going on in his mouth.

"*Polpetto*!" He made a sound of gastric happiness. "Try it, Kayla. It's deliciously fresh. You've never had anything like it."

Yeah, and I really didn't want to start now. I realized my earlier mistake of thinking Paolo was serving us *polenta*. Whole different thing. Cornmeal, not octopus. Cornmeal I could handle. I took one look at the baby octopus in my soup—poor dead baby animal. Was its mother mourning it?—covered my mouth, and ran for the restroom to hurl.

After some minutes of clutching the porcelain throne, the nausea disappeared as quickly as it had come. I felt pale and shaken, but much better. As I cleaned myself up I wondered, *How am I going to explain* this?

Jus startled me as I came out of the bathroom. "You okay?"

I jumped and clutched my heart. "Jus. You scared me. Do you always lurk in doorways by the ladies' room?"

"Sorry." He looked contrite and embarrassed. "I was worried about you."

"I'm fine. It's sweet of you to be concerned." I stroked his cheek and smiled. It was a good thing I was becoming such a fine actor. "Sudden nauseous migraine," I lied. "It came on just like this." I snapped my fingers. "By the time I realized I was getting an aura and my eye hurt, it was too late."

"I didn't know you got migraines."

Neither did I. My freshman roommate at the sorority used to get them. I was borrowing her history, and symptoms, so to speak. "I don't get them like this often. Maybe a couple of times a year? It happens when I'm off schedule."

Maybe I should have given them a little more frequency. An excuse in the hand...

His brow creased. He really was adorably sweet. "Should I take you back to the *pensione*?"

"No. Once I've..." I cleared my throat, indicating delicacy. "The worst is over." I took his hand, which was warm and comforting as it squeezed mine. "How offended is Paolo? Will you explain?"

Jus nodded. "My brothers are having a field day with your squeamishness. I'll put them in their places, too." He sounded like he relished the thought.

"Go gentle on them. Forgive them for what they don't know."

Paolo took it all with good humor and offered me ice for my head, insisting it would help. "It's the bad air in the heat."

Jus translated it for me and whispered, "Italians always complain about the bad air."

After dinner, Diana asked me to take a picture of her and Kirk and the boys. As they jostled into their usual family picture formation, Jus was suddenly nearly as tall as his brothers.

From either side of him, Jerod and Jeremy grabbed a shoulder to push him down. "Off your toes, squirt."

"Justin Arnold Green! Behave yourself. At least you finally reached six feet. Your regular height will suffice. Get off your toes," Diana barked. I wouldn't want to be on the receiving end of her reprimands. "And if anyone starts the lean, I will personally kill them."

Justin's grin was wide and contagious as he and his two brothers started leaning to the right.

Diana swatted at them. I stifled a laugh at their family antics. Being an only child, I didn't have any siblings to joke around with. I'd always wanted big brothers. I was falling in love with Justin's family already. *Boys!* I snapped the picture.

# CHAPTER FIVE

*Justin*

Something was wrong with Kay. Sure, she protested she was fine. But the sudden virulent headache was worrying. Paolo might have been right about the bad air. After sleeping all afternoon, she went straight to bed when we got home from Paolo's.

She blamed it on the headache. "It makes me tired, both before and after. I should have recognized it coming on from how tired I was before."

I sat in the chair in the room of our *pensione*, with my laptop open. I'd looked up her symptoms. Fatigue and nausea were common symptoms. I would just have to take her at her word that this would pass.

As I checked my email, I got a text that made my pulse race.

*You've been ignoring me, hubby. Not interested in playing my game? You should be, baby. I have more pictures you should be interested in. Don't make me use them. I'll be in touch soon.*

I smiled, slowly, and willed my heart to stop racing. Maybe I should have been scared. But I'd been waiting for her.

*Bring it on, baby. Send me a sample of what you have so I can find you.*

I texted Dex.


*Kayla*

*Scrum, scrum, scrum, scrum.*

After a day of watching rugby, the words pulsed through my head in a chant. What better way to pass the time than watching hot guys in shorts tackle each other? Guys flashing very fine butts at the crowd. Male physicality! I needed to fan myself, and it wasn't just due to the heat of the day. Pregnancy hormones should really have made men look worse rather than better to me.

I'd also seen a new side to Jus. Kirk hadn't exaggerated. Jus really did know the game better than anyone. With his powers of observation and strategic thinking, he was an excellent coach.

Jus looked adorable, and hot, as he ran up and down the sidelines yelling at his players, calling plays, sketching them out. He knew his Dad's playbook by heart. He was so intense! And he claimed he didn't like sports all that much.

I played water girl and general helper. And good luck charm. When the guys won their first game under Justin's tutelage, they let me douse them with the water bottles. After they won their second game of the afternoon, they invited me out drinking with them.

"Sorry, boys. I have a date with the coach."

"Tomorrow!" the guys agreed. "We're going to get you out on the field, Kayla!"

One of them winked at me. "Can hardly wait to tackle you, baby."

It was a good thing Jus didn't hear that. At the end of the day, Jus took me by the hand and led me off the field. "I should have known Mom and Dad would put us to work." He was sweaty and scowling.

I laughed at him. "It was fun. Your family has a great business."

"Yeah?" He broke into a grin. "Well I'll be damned if I hang around and get recruited to babysit the players tonight. I'm taking my wife out for dinner."

I made a face. "Not for fish again, I hope? I kind of like my fish cleaned before they're cooked. And shrimp shelled and deveined."

He laughed. "How does pizza sound? Napoli is famous for their own brand of thin-crust pizza. I know the best place. Across the bay in Sorrento. Want to escape with me?"

"If you're going to feed me pizza, I'm in!"

*Justin*

Kayla laughed as I pulled her by the hand through the dark, narrow alleyways of Sorrento. The pizzeria I was taking her to sat at the end of a narrow street that ended at the bay. It had a back terrace that looked across the water toward the sparkling lights of Naples. And hand-tossed, oven-fired pizza that melted in the mouth.

"I hope you know where you're going!" she said. "This area looks sketchy."

"No, it's fine. Just old. If we follow the light to the end of the alley we can't go wrong."

Inside the pizzeria, the atmosphere was pure old country. A nearly wall-sized painting of a jester during *carnivale*, dressed in full ruffles and mask as he put a pizza in the oven, hung on the wall opposite us. The air was filled with the scent of baking bread. I asked to be seated on the open-air brick terrace.

My timing was perfect. The sun was in the process of setting and the moon was rising silver over Vesuvius. We were given a view table. Strings of white lights crisscrossed and sparkled over our heads and the patio. We sat side by side on the same side of the table so we could both enjoy the view. On a bench seat with our backs to a brick wall that was slowly giving up its heat. A large, open window of the pizzeria released delicious aromas to the terrace. A bottle filled with a red rose sat in the middle of the table, along with an unlit candle. A local band played Italian folk music and love songs on the far side of the terrace from us.

I was high on the success of my team that afternoon. We were advancing to the semifinals. I was also high on the adrenaline of the hunt. Damn that ID thief for threatening me. I was tense with both excitement and fear. If I kept ignoring her, would she make good on her threat? Did she have something I wanted? Or was she bluffing?

I wanted her picture so I could flush her out. I needed more data points on her facial structure to hunt her down and shut her off. She was going to make a mistake soon. I could feel it the way I could feel it when my business competition, or a needy supplier, was about to make a desperate move.

I was also high on Kay. As she sat next to me, her new Italian perfume teased my nose. I could feel her body heat next to me. Her breast skimmed my arm, driving me mad with lust.

She was gorgeous, perfect as she studied the menu before her and laughed. "It's useless! Pointless. Like I can read Italian! I have no idea what this menu says. Except for the word pizza. Order me a cheese pizza, will you?" Her eyes danced.

"Cheese, huh?" I teased. "Adventurous as a five-year-old?"

She shoulder-bumped me. "I hear it's a specialty here. Nothing like a kid's pizza at home."

"I'm hungry. We'll need more than one pizza. What else do you want?"

"Anything served without eyes, legs, or shells," she said deadpan. "And no caviar, either. Fish eggs." She shuddered.

"You're no fun." I bumped her back. "But because you were such a good sport today, your wish is my command." I ordered two pizzas and a bottle of red wine.

"Keep the staff happy, is that it?" she said.

"Always."

Couples sat all around us. As if she was taking their cue, she looped her arm through mine and rested her head on my shoulder, gazing at the sunset, and the view.

I'd pulled out the big guns and picked this particular pizzeria for its romantic atmosphere and view as much as for the pizza. My brothers had always taken their girls here. If it was good enough for the Casanovas of my family, why not for me?

My love for Kay danced on the tip of my tongue, silenced by fear of rejection. I whispered to her, "I like what you're doing, but you don't have to act here. No one knows me or us."

She smiled lazily. "I'm doing this for my own pleasure, Jus. I like being out with you."

My heart lurched.

"I'm growing used to this act." She squeezed my arm.

I grinned, trying not to show how happy she made me as a waiter lit the candle on our table.

"Italy has been wonderful so far," she said. "You spoiled me rotten in Milan."

"Not so rotten, I hope," I said. "I had to bribe you before I subjected you to days with my family."

"I don't know why you were worried about it. I love your family!"

I stared at her. "You do?"

"Cross my heart." She laughed. "They're loud and sporty—"

"And you fit in with them better than I do. The stork left me on the wrong doorstep."

"No!" She shook her head. "You don't give yourself enough credit. You were awesome today. I think it made me hot watching you coach your guys. Bossing those big, strong jocks around like that." She pretended to swoon. "Directing the game. Calling the shots. You were brilliant! They couldn't have won without you."

Did she know how hard she was tugging my heart?

I shrugged, trying to appear humble. "Dad could have done just as well. He's coached his team well."

"You're too modest." She sighed. "I like you as warrior leader."

The waiter arrived with our wine and poured us each a glass. I raised mine to Kay's. "To always winning. Chin-chin!"

"Chin-chin!" She looked radiant and happy.

An older Italian couple sat next to us, smiling at the sight of us, their table so close it was almost an extension of ours. The woman turned to me, pointed to our rings, commented on how new and shiny they were, and asked in Italian, "Newlyweds?"

I answered her and was soon carrying on a conversation with her and her husband.

"Yes, we're American."

"Where from? Seattle. Yes, very far away from New York. The opposite side of the country."

"On our honeymoon? Of sorts. She's meeting my family," I explained. "No, my wife doesn't speak Italian."

"Look at the way your wife looks at you!" the woman said. "She adores you! She's very much in love with you. Don't take it for granted. You should tell her you love her often. Women like to hear it. Don't they, my husband?" She smiled at the older man.

My heart beat double time. Had the woman seen something I was blind to? Did Kay love me? Or had she perfected her act?

"Yes, my love." The man reached across the table and took his wife's hand in his. "I tell her always. You tell your wife always and you'll have a long and happy marriage. Like us!" He raised his wine glass to us. "*Salute!*"

*To our health.*

I raised my glass. "*Salute!*"

Kay watched us, an amused, confused look on her face.

Our pizzas arrived. Both tables drifted back into private conversation.

"You're so hot when you're speaking Italian," Kay purred in my ear. "What did they say?"

"Nothing much. Just small talk."

"Jus!" She glanced at the woman. "She's motioning to you. What does she want?"

"The Italians talk too damn much with their hands." I grinned. "She wanted me to tell you something." I wanted to tell her the same thing. Had since college.

"Well? What are you waiting for? Tell me." Her eyes sparkled in the fading light.

I shook my head. "She's mistaken. You don't want to hear it." Not from me. I took a slice of pizza.

Kay slapped my arm. "You can't tease me like that and not *tell* me."

I shrugged.

"Jus! Tell me already."

I set my pizza down, looked earnestly into her eyes, and told her what was in my heart. In Italian, of course. "*Sei il mio tesoro d'oro. Ti voglio bene. Ti amo con tutto il cuore.*"

The Italians are flowery. They would never stoop to just saying a plain *I love you*. Bah! They must embellish. If not, what's the use of being known for their passionate natures?

I learned this from the many Italian rugby players I'd met over the years. You must woo the girl with your words. I'd taken a lesson from them and repeated the Italian way to tell a woman you love her. *You're my golden treasure. I love you. I love you with all my heart.*

And then I kissed her, thoroughly.

The woman I'd been talking to smiled at me. And gave me the Italian equivalent of a thumbs-up, the sweeping arm gesture with her pointer finger making a circle with her thumb, her other fingers extended, meaning *perfect*!

I nodded back.

Kay stared at me, her eyes wide. Her lips moist and plump from my kiss. "In Italian? Really, Jus?"

"You said it was sexy." I picked my pizza up again and took a bite.

"What did you say?"

"Exactly what I meant," I said.

The band that had been quietly playing in the background, interrupted. "*Scusi.* We are now taking requests."

"*Luna Mezza Mare!*" An obviously American man a few tables away called out and pointed to the sky where a full moon was rising.

"Moon over the sea!" The lead singer clicked his tongue in approval. "Very good suggestion from the Americano! A favorite of ours. Who can resist a good *Napolitano* tune about the sea? And the moon. And the love?" He shrugged comically. "Or the lust." He nodded to his band. "One, two, three."

He broke into the first verse of the upbeat song full of innuendo about woman's lovers coming and going.

Kay clapped. "I know this one! You texted me the YouTube link. It's from *The Godfather.*"

"It was in *The Godfather.* But it was popular long before that. It was supposedly written by a *Napolitano* sailor."

The singer left his perch at the end of the terrace and started working the crowd, encouraging the audience to clap along as he sang his way from table to table. The crowd ate it up.

When he stopped at our table, Kay laughed and covered her face with her hand, fingers spread, as the young Italian singer crooned to her. He pulled her hand from her face and held it over his heart while she laughed. She was blushing when he finally released it and stood, clapping his hand against the other one that held the mic.

"*Tutti!*" he yelled, still clapping. *All.* He encouraged the audience to sing along.

Kay nudged me. "Jus, sing! You have to!"

I shrugged. Damn, I wasn't letting that Italian steal my thunder or my girl. I started belting out the lyrics in Italian, keeping up the singer.

He shot me an exaggerated look of surprise and handed the mic to me. I took it and serenaded Kay, breaking into English for just one line that told her there was only one guy she should marry. And that was me. I pointed to myself.

She laughed and clapped as the singer and I broke into a round of la, la, la, la, las. He grabbed me and motioned to follow him to the next table and then join him on stage.

I should have sat back down. But I was having too much fun. My brothers hogged the spotlight at the tourney. Here I was able to be myself and shine. Kay blew me a kiss like a groupie. The older Italian woman at the table next to us leaned over and whispered something to her. Kay nodded, listening intently as she clapped to the song.

Her hands froze in place. Her eyes went wide. Kay's smile became effervescent. Her eyes sparkled in all the light that fell on them—the moonlight, the candlelight, the light from the window behind her. What had the Italian woman said to her?

The song ended to a raucous round of applause. I took a bow and made my way back to Kay, waving and shaking hands. Taking ribbing and teasing. At the table, I slid in next to Kay and put my arm around her.

She turned and smiled at me. "*Ti voglio bene.*"

My heart stopped. I glanced at the older woman. My mouth went dry.

"This isn't part of our act." Kay's voice was soft and full of emotion. "I mean it, Jus. I *love* you."

If hearts could sing, mine was playing an arena right then. "*Sei la mio coccola.* I love you, too.

She stroked my beard. "I have no idea what the first part meant."

"It's something romantic. It doesn't translate exactly—"

She took my face in her hands. "I love you, too. Why didn't you tell me in English the first time?"

"Isn't it obvious?" I swallowed hard.

She smiled softly. "Love makes you vulnerable, Jus. Always has. I—"

I stared at her, waiting for her to finish. "Yes?"

"I think it's time we finished our pizza and went back to the *pensione*. That song you sang to me!" She fanned herself.

I signaled the waiter for the check.

# CHAPTER SIX

*Kayla*

Jus loved me. And I loved him. Stunning and surprising as it was, I really, truly did. Without doubt now, I was in love with Justin Green. Who ever would have thought it possible?

There was something poetic and beautiful about our little scene in the Italian restaurant last night. And about an older Italian woman, an eavesdropper, no less, prompting Jus to confess his secret love for me. And the woman teaching me how to say I love you in Italian. *Ti voglio bene.* Words to live by.

I'd almost told Jus about the baby right then. But to blurt out that kind of news so quickly on the heels of *I love you* seemed crass and calculated. As if I'd been waiting to spring it on him until he declared his undying love and called me his treasure. Not that I ever expected to be called a golden treasure, not even with my blond hair. No, I had *gold digger* attached to my name and reputation. I didn't want Jus thinking I'd been waiting for him to commit before I dropped the bombshell and reeled him, and his wallet, in.

He loved me. But did that mean he wanted to spend the rest of his life with me? He hadn't committed to making the marriage long term. And why should he? In his mind he still had ten months to let this love grow and see where it went. Why rush things?

I wasn't sure myself. I only knew I wanted us to have a fighting chance. I tried to dream up some romantic way to tell him. I came up blank. Was there a romantic way to spring an unplanned pregnancy on a guy?

His birthday. Maybe his birthday. If I was still pregnant on his birthday, August $22^{nd}$, I would definitely tell him. What do you get the guy who has everything? A child, of course!

No, well, in addition. Jus had been struggling so much with colors in Milan. Wouldn't his life be easier and richer if he could see the world as everyone else saw it? I'd saved the results of his online colorblind test, which would allow me to order the correct glasses for him. I made a note to order him a pair of colorblind correction glasses when we got home. The gift of color and a baby. How would any woman ever top that? Who could be more of a golden treasure?

The Greens shepherded around one hundred "young men," to use Diana's words. They had staff that translated for them and got them to all the places they were supposed to be. Staff that coached. Medics and trainers. Administrators to deal with passport and visa issues. A large, happy family of employees, all of them dressed in the signature black rugby shorts and shirts with the Rugby Explorers logo plastered everywhere. And, yes, shouldn't their color have been green? Or was that too obvious?

Jus left early to help his dad with the morning practice. I'd been so sleepy, again, that he'd let me linger in bed. Diana had left a women's outfit for me with a note that it was a gift for me to keep. But please wear it while helping out around camp. She also left me a nametag on a lanyard.

In Milan, I'd gotten used to having a brioche and cappuccino in the bar for breakfast. I missed the simple ritual as I grabbed a pastry and headed to the practice field to find Jus, pulling a cooler full of iced water and sports drink Diana insisted I take to them.

After being catcalled and propositioned by half a dozen Italian men on my way to the field as I struggled with the cooler—blonds were rare in *Napoli*—and having my butt pinched in the process, I found Jus. Kirk, Jerod, and Jeremy were with him, drilling the guys and running them through warmups.

Jus waved to me as I arrived at the sidelines, pulling my red cooler. Kirk let the guys take a water break, to much cheering. They descended on me, joking and flirting while I handed out beverages. Suddenly I was their angel of mercy. And hydration, apparently.

I kissed Jus quickly. There was an emotional intimacy between us now that hadn't been there before. Confidence in us. And a burning passion stronger than any I'd felt before. What I'd had with Eric felt like a pale imitation compared to this. A mere schoolgirl crush. An immature thing. Being with Jus was headier than anything I'd known.

"Kayla, you going to cheer us on today?" one of the players, Matt, said to me as he grabbed a dripping bottle of water. Matt was probably twenty. And just so darn cute.

"I certainly am!" I did a quick cheerleader jump. "Will that do?"

Matt and his buddies clapped. "You ever play any rugby?"

Matt was the biggest flirt of any of the guys. The way he said it was a challenge.

"No." I shook my head. No way I was letting a challenge go unanswered. I was dying to get on the field and give the game a try. "I usually prefer to give blood the old-fashioned way. Played a little lingerie football in college, though. We called it powder puff, but..." I winked. "Don't suppose there's any such thing as lingerie rugby?"

Matt grinned and pulled off his shirt, revealing rock-hard abs. "Let's invent it. I'm game. And damn if I'd mind being known as the inventor of another lingerie sport."

The guys hooted.

I shouldn't have been teasing and flirting with the guys. I was just so happy. I couldn't stop myself. I was wearing a sports bra beneath my rugby shirt. I stripped my shirt off to reveal my sexy bright pink sports bra with a zipper in front and extra underwire. "College lingerie football is always flag. I don't suppose there's such a thing as flag rugby, either? No flag, no game."

Jus came up behind me. "Kay—"

Jerod grabbed a bottle of water from me. "No flags. Sorry, Kayla. How about a promise from the boys to be gentle with you? No tackling the coach's wife. That's just bad form." He put his arm around me, dwarfing me.

In my tennis shoes, I came up approximately to Jerrod's armpit.

"Who's in?" Jerod said.

Someone grumbled, "Where's the fun in that?"

Matt's hand shot up first. A dozen other guys volunteered.

Jus shook his head. "Kay, this is a bad idea." He flicked a gaze at his team. "These brutes get carried away when they're playing. They don't know their own strength—"

"Chill, baby bro." Jeremy took my arm and led me to the field.

After watching an entire day of the game, I knew the basic rules and some of the rudimentary plays.

I rubbed my hands together. "I can hardly wait to be in the scrum!"

"You're not going to be in the scrum with those guys' arms all around you and their hands on your butt." Jus shook his head. "You're too small. You could snap your neck. You're playing wing. Stand outside the scrum and wait to get the ball."

Jerod shook his head and rolled his eyes.

The guys picked quick teams and formed up—shirts and bare chests. I was with the bare chests, though technically I was wearing a sports bra. Jerod was shirts. Jeremy was on my team.

"Aren't you playing, Jus?" I asked, hoping he would.

"Jus never plays, do you, buddy?" Jerod laughed. "He's afraid of getting his ass kicked."

Jus shrugged. Water off a duck's back. "Someone has to ref. I'm the best damn one we've got."

Jus took my arm. "Kay, I wish you wouldn't. The guys get carried away out there. The game's played largely without pads. You don't know how to fall and take a tackle. Every one of those guys outweighs you by a hundred pounds or more—"

I kissed Jus to shut him up. "I'll be fine. This will be fun! Put the ball in play."

Rugby was a complicated game, similar, yet different from American football. The other team kicked off. On the second play, Jeremy got the ball and ran for a try. In rugby, you actually have to touch the ball to the ground after crossing the goal line.

The boys were being a little too protective of me, keeping me out of the action. We kicked off and recovered the ball on the next play. Wanting to show them girls could play, I surged forward and begged for the ball. To my surprise, Matt threw it to me. I caught it, tucked it in close to my right side, and sprinted toward the goal line.

Defenders closed in on me, surrounding me from all sides. I looked behind me for a teammate to throw the ball to and caught a glimpse of a defender in the corner of my eye. I veered right and slammed into a wall of muscle at full speed. I bounced back and lost my footing. I fell too fast. I tucked the ball to protect it and came down hard on it on the hard-packed ground.

I landed with a sickening oomph. I felt a searing pain in my chest. The wind rushed out of me. I gasped for air and couldn't breathe. I was vaguely aware of a lot of swearing going on around me.

*My baby. My baby. My baby. Have I killed my baby?*

Jus was calling my name. My ears rang. I blacked out.

When I came to, Jus was kneeling over me on one side, cradling my head, wearing a passionately worried expression. "Fuck, Jerod! I told you not to hurt her." I'd never heard Jus so angry and upset.

"I'm sorry, Justin. I'm sorry. I didn't mean for it to happen. She ran straight into me. I couldn't get out of the way in time. How is she?"

A forest of guys towered over me, completely dead silent. Like someone had died.

One of the trainers, Sam, was on my other side. "She's coming to. Give her room, guys. She needs air. Kayla? Kayla, can you hear me?"

I nodded and panicked. It hurt so much to breathe. "Can't breathe."

"It's okay. Be calm. You've taken a fall. Try to breathe slowly and as deeply as you can."

"It hurts." I couldn't help myself. I whimpered. The pain was so intense. My lungs ached. I couldn't get a full breath of air. I started crying. I caught a glimpse of a first-aid bag out of the corner of my eye.

"I'm going to examine you," Sam said. "I'll try to be gentle, but it may hurt. Is that okay?"

I nodded. "Jus!" I cried. I needed Jus.

Jus took my hand and squeezed it. "I'm here. I'm right here, babe."

"Can't breathe." I could barely see him through the tears I was trying to hold back.

"I know." He stroked my forehead incredibly gently, brushing the hair off my face. "I'm going to unzip your sports bra. That may help." He looked at the trainer. "Bruised ribs?"

Sam nodded. "Or cracked."

I yelped, just a little, as Jus tugged the zipper down and the pressure on my lungs eased only minimally. The zipper was for extra support. When it was unzipped, it exposed more fabric, not a lot more of me. Not that I was worried about modesty. I clutched my stomach, wondering if I'd just gotten my wish and would soon be unpregnant, and held back a flood of tears. Suddenly, I wanted Justin's baby. Fickle is woman.

Sam probed my ribcage. I knew he was trying to be gentle, but I thought I was going to pass out again at the pain. "Her ribcage isn't distended. It doesn't look like she's broken anything. Maybe cracked a few. Impossible to tell without an x-ray."

"No x-ray!" I murmured, thinking of the baby.

Jus stroked my forehead again. "No, no x-ray. It wouldn't do any good anyway. There's nothing a doctor can do for a cracked rib except diagnose it."

I heard the rip of an instant icepack.

"She came down hard on that ball. She's bruising already." Sam pointed, outlining my ribcage in the air. "You know the drill, Justin. Ice on, ice off every fifteen to twenty. Over-the-counter anti-inflammatory pain-killers like ibuprofen for the pain. Rest. Lots and lots of rest. Three- to four-week recovery time. Maybe longer. No strenuous activity."

A tear slid down my cheek. I was still clutching my abdomen. The pain radiated everywhere. I couldn't tell what was what. I kept expecting to feel a warm rush of blood while I miscarried. But so far, nothing. I couldn't ask Sam. Not without Jus knowing. Why hadn't I told him? I had to tell him.

My head was fuzzy. I couldn't think clearly. I was going to tell. *On his birthday. That's right. On his birthday.*

"She's clutching her stomach." Jus sounded worried as he looked at Sam. "What does that mean?"

Sam leaned over me and gently applied the icepack. "Kayla, does your abdomen hurt?"

"Can't tell. Everything hurts." I tried to take a deep breath and whimpered again. I was such a baby.

"I think she's fine," Sam said to Jus. "Rupturing something would be unusual. Take her home and watch her. Make sure she rests propped up. See if Diana has a wedge pillow. You know what to look for." Sam turned to me. "It's going to hurt to breathe for a while, Kayla.

But it's important to fill your lungs with as much air as possible. Even though it hurts, try to breathe deeply."

I nodded. Everyone looked so worried. I tried to joke. "Easy for you to say."

Jus shot a death glare at Jerod.

"It's okay, Jerod," I said. "I ran into you. Did I dent you? Did I hurt you?"

"Nothing hurts me, sweetheart. I'm fine," Jerod said. "Hang tough, kiddo. I've had my share of bruised and cracked ribs. They hurt like hell for a while. But they heal fast if you take care of yourself."

Jus interrupted. "I'm taking her home." He scooped me up into his arms. As he stood, I wrapped one arm around his neck, held the icepack against me with the other, and laid my head against his chest, listening to the strong, reassuring beat of his heart. A heart that beat for me.

# CHAPTER SEVEN

*Kayla*

As soon as we got back to the *pensione*, I made an excuse to use the bathroom. It hurt tremendously to move. But I wasn't bleeding. I still had the baby. And suddenly, the thought made me incredibly happy. Now that my pregnancy had been threatened, I wanted it more than anything. Some people tried forever to get pregnant. We accidentally fell into it. Maybe we were going to have a brood of children. I didn't know. But no matter what happened, I wanted this one.

Jus settled me in bed and propped up with all the pillows he could find. Dosed me with painkillers. And let me sleep. That night, he slept in the chair so he wouldn't disturb me.

I stayed in bed the rest of that day and the next and slept. It hurt to breathe. It hurt to laugh. It hurt to cough. And it really hurt to hurl. Morning sickness and cracked ribs were an absolutely painful combination. And hiding the hurling became even more difficult.

I didn't get much better in a day and a half. But I didn't get worse. Sam said that was key. It turned out bruised ribs were the perfect cover for most of the symptoms of pregnancy. So there was that. I could sleep all I wanted. Was even encouraged to.

Diana wasn't the nurturing kind. She was the type of mom who simply told you to buck up and bear it. She had no time to baby people. But she was sympathetic in her own way, making sure I iced my ribs on a regular schedule, and always had plenty of cold icepacks. And plenty to drink. Hydration was key. I wondered where Jus had gotten his sweet, nurturing nature from. How had he survived being a small, sickly, nonathletic child in this family?

Being around his brothers, I'd seen firsthand how they picked on him and teased him. I supposed it was natural for big brothers to be that way. But I could also see how Jus didn't appreciate it. Or still being considered the baby when he'd surpassed all of them financially and was something of a shark in the business world. I wondered if his ambition and drive stemmed partly from a sense to prove himself. If so, it appeared to me to be a losing battle. Birth order was immutable. And so was physical stature. No matter how rich, important, or powerful Jus became, he was always going to be baby bro to Jerod and Jeremy.

Who were spoiling me rotten, along with Matt and the rest of the players. I hadn't had so much male attention since I'd be the Beauty of Tau Psi in college, the fraternity's yearly princess. The guys brought me news of the tourney, regaled me with their teams' exploits and videos of tournament play, and tried to fatten me up with an ever-growing variety of gelato.

It became something of a joke and a game with them. The first day I was hurt, nothing sounded good. They tried to tempt me with everything they could think of to get me to eat something. I swore they'd all picked up some Italian mamma tendencies. "You're too-a skinny! Eat-a something, kiddo!"

Finally sea salt caramel gelato did the trick. I gobbled down an entire bowl of it. Fortunately, I'd stopped short of asking for pickles with it. After that, I was deluged with sea salt caramel everything. And a tempting assortment of gelato in an attempt to give me variety in my diet.

"At least she loves something from the sea," Jerod had said with a tease in his eyes. He'd been so sweet to me. Deep down he was a lot like Jus. Just more macho on the outside.

Like Jus, he and Jeremy liked to tease and prank.

He was so much like Jus that way—it was clear what devilment he was contemplating. I tilted my head and shook my finger at him. "Don't you dare try to bring me baby octopus ice cream!"

"*Polpetta gelato*! Never even crossed my mind. I'll have to suggest that. I was thinking more of a topping. Wouldn't a cute, little baby octopus be delicious perched on top instead of a cherry?" He laughed. "Wouldn't dare. Baby bro would use his gray matter to think up a diabolical way to kill me. Either that or give all my electronic devices a virus I'd never get rid of.

"Word of advice—don't get on his bad side. He holds a grudge."

I frowned. "He's still upset with you? I've explained a dozen times. *I* ran into *you*! Not the other way around. And then I lost my footing and fell on the ball. It was an accident, pure and simple. Part of the game. Contact sports involve risk. And, um, contact." I laughed and immediately winced because it hurt so bad.

Jerod was sitting in a chair pulled close to my bed. "Oh, he knows that." He winced, too, out of sympathy. "Sorry. I've had my share of bruised ribs. I know what it's like."

"That's all right. It only hurts when I breathe, laugh, or cough." I tried to take a deep breath of air like Sam had insisted. But it hurt worse than anything. "I'll keep on him."

Jerod patted my hand and grinned. "Good luck with that. He's pissed. He had a romantic honeymoon trip down the coast planned, complete with a couple of days on a yacht with nothing planned but ogling you in your bikini and lots of sex. Now he's not going to get to bone you the way he'd planned."

"Who says he's not?" I said.

Jerod shook his head and laughed. "You're a braver girl than I thought. Then again, any girl who'll do it with Jus deserves a medal." He winked. "Oh, ouch! No.

Not there. That hurts. Careful! Watch the ribs." He shook his head. "Not the noises a guy wants to hear. Maybe okay for some guys. But Justin is the sensitive type. Too much pressure not to hurt you to really enjoy the act."

He patted my hand again. "You need to give yourself time to rest and recuperate. Don't push it. Justin can wait. He has plenty of money to take you on a trip another time. He just needs time to get over his disappointment.

"My brother isn't a selfish prick. He's already making noises about taking you home. He'd wanted to fly you back to Seattle immediately. Mom had to convince him to let you rest here a few days first." Jerod paused. "I joke around and tease Justin a lot. But he's a good guy."

High praise from Justin's older brother.

On Sunday, the tourney ended. July had slid into August. Italy shut down for the month. Diana, Kirk, Jerod, Jeremy, and the team were preparing to leave Naples for home on Tuesday. As far as I knew, our honeymoon was still on. Jus hadn't told me any differently.

Jus came into my room, sat gently on the bed, and took my hand in his. "I've arranged for a jet. I'm taking you home tomorrow. You need your rest to heal."

He looked adorably sad and disappointed. His face was set. I'd seen that look before. There was no use arguing the point.

I didn't have the energy anyway.

Jerod had been right on target about what Jus would do.

"I'm sorry." I took Justin's hand. "This is my fault. If I hadn't insisted on playing—"

He cut me off with a kiss. "It's no one's fault. We can't live in a bubble."

That sounded like something Diana would say.

"I'm disappointed." I batted my eyes and put on a pout, trying to get a smile from him. "And really sorry this isn't the honeymoon we both wanted." He hadn't even seen me naked in three days. And I'd been pretty comatose most of the time, anyway.

"How's the injury?"

I lifted my shirt to show him my bruises, which were in full bloom now. Black, purple, and scary. "Ugly."

He grimaced and turned away. "Damn, Kay. They're getting worse."

"It took a few days for the deep ones to surface." I put my shirt down.

"I could kill Jerod."

"That's what he said." I looked him in the eye. "You have to forgive him. It's not his fault."

"I know. I have." He took a deep breath. "But seeing you hurt like this." He shook his head. "This is some shitty romantic trip I've taken you on."

I shook my head. "Jus. This is the best trip I've ever had. That night at the pizzeria when you told me you loved me." Tears welled in my eyes. "It was the most beautiful moment of my life."

He looked almost startled.

"Way more romantic than when you proposed." I tried to say it with a straight face.

He laughed. "Yeah. That was something we both can only imagine."

I laughed and grabbed my side. "Ouch. Don't make me laugh!" I took as deep a breath as I could. "After I heal—"

He took my hands in his. "I'll make it up to you. I'll take you anywhere you want."

I leaned forward for a kiss. "Anywhere you are is fine with me."

His answering smile was radiantly happy. "I love you, Kay."

"In English, even!" I didn't know why that made me so happy. "I love you, too, Jus. So much. Always remember that."

I didn't know why I felt the need to warn him, but I had a strange foreboding. Maybe it was the uncertainty of being pregnant and keeping it from him. I was too perfectly happy. I wanted to hang on to this moment forever. Even though I was in pain. Physical pain was easier to bear than heartbreak. Jus loved me! Now if he reacted well to the news of the baby...

*Kayla*

How to tell Jus he was going to be a daddy. How to tell him? How to *tell* him!

We celebrated two months of "marriage" quietly at home on the Wednesday evening after we got back. Over a dinner Magda had made that was supposed to be good for the blood and help me heal. Only, it wasn't exactly two months of "marriage" for me. I'd come into this marriage four days late.

When I pointed that out to Jus, he laughed. "Does that mean you want me to adjust *my* anniversary by four days? Controlling woman! How will we explain that?" His eyes twinkled.

"You're a billionaire," I said. "You can do whatever eccentric thing you want. Have two anniversaries four days apart if you like." I paused, screwing up my courage. "By the way, as a matter of semantics, isn't an anniversary supposed to be a yearly event?"

Jus just grinned. "Yeah. Come to think of it."

My heart skipped a beat. Was he thinking of making this permanent? Was he hinting at it? Or was I reading way too much into things? Would he still be thinking of it when I told him my news?

I almost blurted it out right then. The two-month mark was a good milestone. Something to celebrate. As Jus had pointed out on the plane home, sixty days were over now. Almost all the surveillance tapes would have been overwritten. Just a very small percentage left, if any. Once ninety days were over, we'd be free and clear of any worry over them...

Maybe I should tell him on day ninety?

No, I couldn't wait that long.

His birthday. I had an appointment with an ob/gyn next week. Once I got the all-clear that everything was well with the pregnancy, *then* I would tell him. On his birthday. In some romantic way. Some way that made him feel like stud of the century! Like his love was so potent that getting me pregnant was inevitable. And highly desirable, of course.

According to the Internet, telling a guy in a romantic way almost always involved giving him your pregnancy test all wrapped up like a gift. Preferably after feeding him. Again, preferably a romantic steak dinner and wine. My own aside here—getting the guy happy and relaxed couldn't hurt.

Because nothing says romance like giving a guy a stick you peed on wrapped in a bow. Especially after they've eaten. Maybe even during dessert over another glass of wine. And hoping he reads those two little pink lines correctly. Especially since the novice daddy-to-be presumably hasn't had the advantage of reading the instructions so he knows what *two* lines mean. As opposed to one or none or thirty-three.

I could just imagine the confused looks he might give. *What the hell is this? Are two lines good or bad? Am I supposed to be happy? Or sad and sympathetic?* Because what guy pays attention to that stuff?

Probably, if you're going to give a guy a pregnancy wand as a gift, just to be clear, you should spring for the one that says "pregnant" in the little window. Which I could always do, and simply retake the test. But why?

Another great suggestion—getting down on one knee like you're proposing and asking him to be your baby daddy with the stick balanced on your fingertips like you're offering him an engagement ring. At that point, wasn't it a little too late? Like, he already was the daddy whether he wanted to be or not. And what if he said no? Talk about an emotional kick to the gut.

Okay, so I was going to keep thinking. Whatever I ended up with, there wasn't going to be any question-asking on my part. No options. Just, *You're going to be a dad, Super Sperm.*

Because, really, I still wondered how his sperm had gotten through. And Jus was just nerdy enough to enjoy the idea of a superpower. Though maybe not so much that it referred to his sperm.

"What do you want to do for your birthday?" I asked him. What were the odds he'd say, *Have a baby with you!*

He shrugged. "There's no need to make a fuss. Something intimate. Last year for my twenty-first I had a huge party. Went to too many bars. After the third bar, I don't remember the rest." He winked.

"Kind of like your wedding," I said, because it was too good an opportunity to pass up. "I'm sensing a theme here." I laughed. "So not a repeat of last year?" I nudged him beneath the table with my foot. "Something you'll remember?" I gave him a hopeful look. "Maybe even forever. Got it. No problem."

He gave me a suspicious look. "What are you planning?"

"Nothing," I said, trying not to give anything away. Maybe I would tell him about the baby over breakfast in bed? Or do the really corny thing and put a cinnamon bun in the oven to heat up for him. And then drag him into the kitchen and point to it there in the oven. And then to my stomach. Until he got the idea.

Jus could be naïve, but he was a quick one. It probably wouldn't take him long.

If that failed, getting a stick I peed on while he ate homey waffles or pancakes was probably better than after a big steak dinner. Less heavy in the stomach when the shock set in. Or the delight. I'd hope for delight.

"Your birthday is a Friday," I said as conversationally and calmly as I could. "Can you take it off?"

He shook his head. "No, babe. Sorry—"

"Meetings," I said before he could finish. "You *will* be in town?"

"Is that a command?"

I nodded. "It is."

"Then yes. I'll make a point of it. I wouldn't dare travel and miss the first birthday I've ever had a girlfriend."

"Girlfriend?" I shook my head. "And here I thought I was your wife."

He laughed.

"Speaking of wives, let's go away for our three months together. Just for a week or so. I'll be healed by then. The fall retail season will have barely begun. The weather will still be good." *And I won't be big as a beach ball yet.* "My big sample sale for the hospital will be over. It's perfect timing."

"When's the sale again?" Jus asked with a tease.

"September fourth." I kicked him playfully. Yes, sometimes I was violent.

He could hardly *not* remember the date of the sale. I reminded him of it constantly, warning him not to go out of town for Flash's, and my, big event. It was his duty, and Riggins', to attend.

"I'll look at my calendar."

I smiled at him, thinking I would get him something special for three months together. Like a wedding cake topper with a bearded groom. I could have one specially made to look like him. Maybe one of those 3-D printing places.

# CHAPTER EIGHT

*Justin*

Friday at work I was alone in my office, head down working, when I got a text from a restricted number. My heart stopped. How sweet. A selfie of the girl I married. The ID-thieving bitch. In my hotel room. Sitting next to me, her head turned, while I was passed out on the bed, a marriage license next to me. She was smart. Still smart enough, at least, not to send me a picture of her face. But she'd made a mistake. This picture was from a different angle than the other two Dex and I had.

*Let's talk,* the text read.

*Not yet,* I thought. *Not until I have you where I want you.*

Adrenaline kicked in. My heart thumped back into action. My pulse raced. The phone shook in my hand. I blew out a breath, trying to control my excitement. Was that what I thought it was?

I enlarged the photo. Yes, identifying marks. A couple of small scars. And the shape of her left eye. People's faces aren't ever symmetrical. One eye is always larger or smaller than the other. Deeper set. Droopier. The same with the mouth and nose. Each half is slightly different. Having the measurements of both sides makes getting a match much more likely. Now we could extrapolate the distance between her eyes, a key measurement we needed. Get a more accurate measurement of the length of her nose. All the data we needed to find her.

I'd just won the spying lottery. Eager and excited. Thrill of the hunt. Could she use this picture to destroy me? I'd bet my lunch money running it through an error-level analyzer would prove it was authentic and unaltered. Too bad for her it didn't prove anything except we'd been in a hotel room together. If she'd acted on this earlier when I'd been unsure of Kay and the existence of surveillance tape, then yeah. But now, as long as Kay swore *she* was the girl at my wedding, I was safe. Dex and I were already implementing a plan that would render the Kay imposter powerless. I just needed a little more time.

Ophie knocked on my office door. I jumped.

"Sorry to startle you, Jus." She'd started calling me Jus after realizing that was what Kayla called me. And putting a flirty flip in her voice at every opportunity.

I should have corrected her. Told her to call me Justin. But after all this time working together, I refused to turn into alpha asshole boss on her now. She'd been with me since the beginning. I gave her more leeway than anyone else. Even Riggins was more formal with me than Ophie. She was treading close to the edge of her line. I hoped I didn't have to rein her in.

"Riggins needs to see you immediately."

Her perfume wafted over to me. Was she wearing Kay's signature scent? It smelled slightly different on her. Not as enticing. What the shit was Ophie up to?

"He asked me to ask you to bring the Smithson presentation and the drawings for the Reno warehouse expansion. He's in his office."

I couldn't criticize her work. She was as efficient, dedicated, and loyal as she had always been. She practically begged to work late hours with me, even when I tried to send her home. Since I'd married Kayla, Ophie had gradually started fixing up more. Wearing more makeup. Dressing in skirts. Getting fashion advice from the merch buyers on the floor. Trying to look a little too similar to Kay. And failing to match her allure.

I preferred the old way Ophie looked. It was funky, nerdy, and cute. I didn't dare tell her that. She took any compliment from me the wrong way—as encouragement. And any criticism of appearance as devastation.

If her familiarity and flirting with me continued, Riggins would have to talk to her. Anything coming from me was a landmine.

The hunger and betrayal in her eyes when she thought I wasn't looking sent a chill down my spine. But there was no way any boss could bring up a look in a woman's eyes as grounds for speaking to an employee. Not without getting his ass sued.

I nodded. "Tell him I'll be right there."

I set my phone down and dug through the paperwork to find the plans Riggins wanted. I grabbed then and my laptop, and headed to find Riggins. I was halfway to his office when I realized I'd left my phone on my desk. I turned around to go back and get it.

Ophie was walking down the hall behind me, holding my phone out to me. "Jus! Hold up. You forgot this!"

Her smile was almost smug. As I took it from her, I couldn't shake the feeling she was spying on me. Damn. My phone was password protected. There was no way she could have read that text from Dex.

### Kayla

I was going to throw Jus a small party. Just a few close friends and family. My parents would want to spend Justin's first birthday as their son-in-law with him. I'd invite my aunt and uncle; Dex's parents, too. Riggins, Lazer, Dex. Britt and a few of the girls to round out the party.

I called caterers and ordered the colorblind correction glasses for Justin in a style of frame I hoped would accentuate the shape and structure of his face. Make him look bookishly nerdy and hot. I ordered a cake from the bakery up the street from Flash.

And then I got a flash of inspiration—ha ha—on how to tell him about the baby. But I needed Britt's help. So between planning like crazy for the benefit sample sale, and stopping by the children's hospital for my weekly visit, I had to take Britt into my confidence.

I took her out to lunch in Bellevue on a Saturday afternoon, far away from Flash so no one we knew would overhear. The media had stopped lurking behind every bush now that the novelty of our marriage had worn off. I wanted to tell her my news in person without a chance of Jus overhearing.

"You are sworn to absolute secrecy." I pointed a finger at her. "On penalty of...of—"

"Of what? Taking back the shoes I borrowed?" Britt laughed. "You're never getting those adorable Jimmy Choos back anyway, and you know it. You can afford a new pair."

She'd lost her awe of me being a billionaire's wife surprisingly quickly. And was right back to being the old Britt who flipped me crap when she wanted. And wasn't good at returning things.

"I'm going to have a baby!" It felt so good to blurt it out to someone I actually knew.

She squealed and hugged me and got a happy tear in her eye. "You took my advice and got pregnant ASAP! Smart girl! Justin is now yours for life. Child support, baby! Child support as insurance should anything go wrong!"

I shook my head. "I knew you'd say that, Britt. You're evil. It's not like that at all."

I was unconsciously playing with my napkin, nervously wringing it. "This wasn't planned. It was an accident." I bit my lip. "I'm worried about how Jus is going to take it."

"He's crazy for you. Walks around with a big grin at the office all the time. Thinks he's a stud now that he's caught you. He's going to be the proudest dad ever. And if he isn't? So what! It's indisputably his, right?"

"You have to ask?" I tried not to sound as indignant as I felt. "Of course it is!"

"Well," she said with a look of the world on her face. "You seemed to have a thing for Lazer going on for a while there."

I waved off her insinuation. "Like I would cheat on Jus!"

Which, of course, I might have in the early days. But that felt like ancient history already.

Britt shrugged. "Jus is yours now. And so is the baby. He's going to have to deal with it."

She sighed deeply and happily. Smugly. "I hope it's a girl, Lala. A pretty blond little girl who looks like you! Justin will adore her. And we'll have so much fun dressing her. She can call me Aunty Britt. I mean, she doesn't have any real aunts, does she?"

I shook my head. "Not yet. Not until Justin's brothers marry."

"I'll be long established as her favorite aunt long before that." Her smile was radiant.

Just then Ophie came around the corner from the direction of the ladies' room. Had she been hiding behind a potted palm and eavesdropping or what? My heart stopped as she approached our table and gave us a big, fake smile.

"Kayla! Britt! Funny running into you here." She seemed both nervous and excited.

I smiled cautiously back at her. "Ophie. What brings you to our part of town?"

"Shopping. For my mom's birthday."

Something about the way she said "birthday" gave me a chill. Ophie lived across the lake in Seattle. Where there was plenty of shopping. Yes, we had the Bravern in Bellevue, with Neiman Marcus and other high-end shops. But it wasn't as if she couldn't have found something in Seattle. We made uncomfortable, stilted small talk for a few minutes before she excused herself.

"I was just on my way out," she said. "Say hi to Jus for me." She gave a little, awkward wave and walked away.

I watched her disappear out the door into the sunshine and suppressed a shudder. "Why do I feel like someone's walked on my grave every time I see her? How is she at work? Still panting after Jus?"

Britt was my spy.

She shrugged. "She thought he was hers. So, yeah. She follows him around like a puppy dog."

I frowned. "I wish I could insist Jus fire her. But he has no grounds and he's fond of her." I grimaced. "And loyal to those who've been loyal to him. Why do I get the feeling she's spying on me? That this 'accidental' meeting was anything but. I wouldn't put it past her to have been skulking around the corner with a cup to her ear. Do you think she overheard anything about the baby?"

Britt shook her head. "How could she? No. It's too noisy in here. She was in the bathroom."

"Supposedly." I stirred my coffee.

"No. We played it cool. There's no way she heard anything. And even if she did, she wouldn't be cheeky enough to spill the news to Justin. What would she have to gain by that?"

But I was thinking about Lazer, too. And what damage she could do with that.

# CHAPTER NINE

*Kayla*

In mid-August in Seattle, the days are suddenly notice-
ably shorter. The shadows are longer. And the marine
air, better known as clouds or fog to everyone else,
comes in in the mornings, giving a preview of fall and
keeping the days cooler.

Justin's birthday, however, dawned clear and blue.
With the promise of heat. I took the clear sunshine and
blue skies as a good omen. I was telling him about the
baby today. Enough of secrets. Things had to be out in
the open if we had any chance of making it as a "married" couple. And this secret wasn't going away.

My doctor had proclaimed I had a healthy pregnancy. All signs pointed to it continuing. Even my fall and
bruised ribs hadn't hurt my developing baby. My grow-

ing fetus was one tough cookie. Which pleased me in an odd way.

I was going to be showing soon. Already my waist was growing thicker. I'd been able to pass it off as coming from inactivity while I healed. But my bruises were almost gone now. Faint hints of yellow and green. And Jus was getting worried that I was still so tired and didn't seem to have much appetite.

Fortunately, I'd only actually hurled on a few inconvenient times. I'd been able to hide my nausea and cravings pretty thoroughly.

So, with ten million dollars on the line, and most importantly my heart and future happiness, I was going to tell my "husband," whom I'd grown to love beyond reason, that he was going to be a father. In the most adorable way I could think of. And, okay, I gave up. It did involve giving him a peed-on wand with two pink bars he'd likely think were gray. If not for my other gift to him. As a last resort, really.

I'd given Magda the morning off. Which she only grudgingly took when I let her put a breakfast feast for Jus in the fridge the night before. With cooking instructions for me to stick in the oven.

I got up early, before Jus, and set the table, complete with presents. And put the breakfast casserole and monkey bread Magda had left for us in the ovens.

I was just putting the finishing touches on the table when Jus strolled in from the bedroom in his boxers, rubbing his eyes. Half naked, he looked hot. I don't know. Love makes a person more attractive, not less.

So maybe Jus still was a little nerdy. But that didn't dim his hotness and appeal. Not in my eyes.

My pulse was leaping with nerves. My stomach in a knot. I hoped this would turn into another "inconvenient rush to the toilet" situation.

"Happy birthday!" I ran to him and threw myself into his arms.

He caught me in a hug and kissed me. "Best birthday ever already! You must be feeling better. You don't wince anymore when I hug you."

"That's just because I love you and think you're totally hot, golden birthday boy," I teased.

"And before I was just a geek," he said with a grin. His dick was hard as he pressed against me.

"An adorable geek who just needed a simple makeover to bring out his real animal magnetism." I kissed him again quickly and tried to pull away.

"Where are you going? Don't tease me. It's customary for the birthday guy to get a birthday boink." His eyes were dark and aroused.

"Absolutely! But there's disagreement among authorities on the subject exactly when during the day is optimum. Mine say after breakfast." I pulled away from him as the oven timer went off, thinking he might refuse that boink after he got the news.

"Hard woman." He saw the table then. "Wow! A birthday table! Is all that for me?" He inhaled deeply. "It smells good in here. Is that monkey bread?" He rubbed his hands together.

I grabbed the oven mitts, put the casserole on the table, and dumped the monkey bread onto a plate. "It is indeed. Your mom said monkey bread has been your favorite since you were little. And it's tradition to make it for you on your birthday."

He was beaming as he took a seat at the table. "Look at these presents."

Yeah. Look at them. I hoped he was still as excited about them once he opened them. I'd pulled out all the stops for this birthday and daddy-to-be reveal. No matter how it went, it was all I could do. I'd done my absolute best.

I poured him a glass of freshly squeezed orange juice and made him a cup of coffee, acting like a domestic goddess as I floated around the kitchen in my silk shorty robe, matching nightgown, and open-toe kitten-heel slippers with feathers across the straps, all in Justin's favorite blue. Which he confused for violet or lavender.

Somehow, I made it through breakfast. Though nerves on top of morning sickness was not fun.

Jus laughed at me. "You're more excited for this birthday than I am."

"I'm just eager for you to open your presents!"

He looked at the small pile of them. "At breakfast? Then I won't have anything to open later."

"You'll have plenty to open later from everyone else." I bit my lip and clenched my hands in my lap to keep them from shaking. "I wanted you to open the gifts from me while we're alone."

"Oh." His eyes lit up with the wrong idea. "In that case, what's first?"

I pointed to the package with the colorblind correction glasses. He opened it, teasingly, slowly, taking great care with the wrapping.

"Just get on with it, Jus! You're not an old lady."

He started folding the wrapping paper like he was going to save it for later and reuse it.

"Jus!" I practically screamed at him. I was so nervous and jumpy. "Stop teasing. We can afford to buy new wrapping paper. You're just being obnoxious."

When he finally got the package open, he pulled the glasses out and stared at them with a puzzled look. "Sunglasses?"

It was clear he didn't understand my excitement. The lenses were light gray. It was easy to confuse them for sunglasses.

I shook my head. "Colorblind correction glasses." I clapped. "What do you give the guy who has everything? The gift of color!"

He frowned, clearly at war with himself. He obviously didn't want to disappoint me by being disappointed with my gift. But he clearly wasn't thrilled. "Kay—"

"I know. I know. You like seeing the world the way you do. But I have a reason for giving them to you. Trust me. I'm hoping the way they change the color of your world will be a good thing. It's never wrong to try to see the world from a different perspective, is it?"

"You've become philosophical now?" He looked both amused and bemused.

"Just open the next one." I pointed, feeling like I was about to toss my cookies—or monkey bread, in this case. Everything hinged on the next gifts. On the revelation they contained. "That one."

*Here goes everything.*

He picked up the box and shook it. "It's in a shirt box. It shakes like a shirt. I'm guessing it's a shirt."

He opened this one more quickly. Probably because he sensed, rightly, that I would slug him if he didn't. Being his birthday wouldn't stop me.

He pulled off the lid and pulled back the tissue. "It is a shirt! A T-shirt." He frowned. On the shirt was a picture of a block of aged cheese with a small piece missing. He read the words on it aloud. "The old block?" He stared at me.

I bit my lip.

"What's this? A tiny T-shirt." His frown deepened. "The chip?" It had a picture of a small chunk of cheese on it.

Okay, it wasn't as tacky as it sounded. Britt had done an excellent job procuring them. They were exactly what I wanted. Funky and cool. Stylish for T-shirts. In top-quality cotton, breathable and comfortable. Organic and chemical free for the baby. And funny on his birthday. Him, at twenty-two, being "the old block."

"Is this part of our new Doggy and Me line?" He held the T-shirt up to Data, who barked happily at his feet, worked up by the excitement.

For a genius, he was kind of slow at this.

"It's part of a new line, all right." I pointed to the last gift. I hated to resort to this. But what could you do? "Before you open it. Put on your new glasses."

He sighed and did as I commanded.

"They make you look sexy and mysterious. Like James Bond or a CIA agent." I folded my hands together and pressed them to my lips.

He stared at me, looking at me with a startled expression. "Kay! Your eyes...and your nightgown and robe...they're...a color I've never seen before."

Oh crap! I hadn't counted on him becoming distracted. He sounded almost upset. Like the world didn't look right.

"Just open the present," I said in a rush. "Don't look anywhere else. Keep your eyes on the contents of the package." I still had my fingers pressed to my mouth so my words came out a little muffled.

He shrugged and opened the box. When he pulled the pregnancy test wand out, he looked at it and at me. "What the hell? What is this?"

"Oh, just something I peed on for you." I laughed. "Yeah, I went all out for your birthday, as you can tell. And gave you a part of myself. Nothing says happy birthday like bodily fluids—"

Understanding was beginning to dawn on him. "Kay—"

"It was important you be able to see pink, Jus. Just this once, you had to be able to see pink. There are two pink lines in the test window. See them? That means the test is positive."

"Chip off the old block?" He paled. And then his face lit up. "Does this mean...?"

"We're going to have a baby, Jus. I don't know how it happened. It was a complete accident. That damn one percent failure rate of the pill—"

He let out a whoop and grabbed me in a hug so tight I thought he was going to bruise my ribs again. "I love you, Kay," he said into my neck.

I felt something wet.

When he pulled away there were tears in his eyes. He put his hand on my abdomen. "I love you both."

I'd never seen him so emotional.

"A baby for my birthday?" He still sounded stunned. "You really did go all out." He paused. "Best birthday ever! When is it due?"


*Justin*

I stared at Kay with new eyes. I was so damned happy! She hadn't just given me the gift of color. Or the gift of fatherhood. She was mine now. It was only natural for me to ask her to be my real wife. Not now. I had to do it in some romantic way. A real proposal. I'd cheated her out of a wedding. She deserved for me to go down on one knee for her.

The clock in the living room chimed.

"Shit! It's late. I have to get to work."

"Time flies when you're having a baby!" Her eyes sparkled.

I gave her another quick kiss and headed to the bedroom to change, still wearing the glasses. In awe of how different the world looked now that I was going to be a dad.

In the closet, my clothes looked different. Seeing color through the glasses, I finally saw what everyone else did. I held up a shirt and pair of pants I used to pair. "These really do clash! When seen through your eyes, you were right."

I took her hand. "Now that I've admitted I was wrong, can a guy get a birthday screw?" I nuzzled her neck, going hard for her. "It won't hurt you...or the baby?"

The baby. I was going to be a father. Shit, that sounded grown-up and odd.

"I thought you were running late?"

"What I have in mind won't take long." I moved her hand to my dick.

"Jus," she said softly. "We've been making love and it hasn't hurt that baby. And you've been so gentle with me, it hasn't hurt me, either." She dropped her robe and slid her nightgown off until she was wearing only a tiny thong panty.

With the glasses on, I could see the faint green tinges of her bruise for the first time. At least, I deduced the color I was seeing was green. "This is a hell of a way to see green for one of the first times." I softly kissed her ribcage, scooped her into my arms, carried her to bed, and made love to the mother-to-be of my child.

On my way to the office, I got a call from Dex.

"Have I got a birthday present for you!" He sounded excited. "The birthday present to top all birthday presents."

I doubted that.

"Dude, we got her! We got everything on her."

The last time I'd heard Dex this excited, we'd won the all-campus college video game tournament.

"What?" I couldn't believe it. This birthday had just run past golden, right on to platinum.

Dex started rattling off details. "Time to put the plan in action." He gave an evil laugh.

At Flash, I could hardly keep my smile down. People thought I was obnoxious about birthdays. I promised Kay not to spill about the baby to anyone until we'd told our parents and family. Britt, however, had helped with my present. She gave me a knowing look and whispered, "Congrats, Papa!" in my ear.

They had cake for me in the cafeteria. And then I was off to a meeting. I missed Kay when she stopped by while she was out running errands. I suspected she'd been to the bakery by Flash to pick up my birthday cake.

Ophie caught me just as I returned to my office. She was waving a phone. "You Greens and your phones! This fell out of your wife's purse, I believe. She's going to need it. She said something about expecting an important text or email or something from the hospital about the sample sale. Shall I have someone run it over to her? I think she said she was heading home from here."

"I'll take it to her." I was too happy to stay in the office. It was my company and my birthday. Why couldn't I take the rest of the afternoon off?

I'd ordered a balloon bouquet and flowers for Kay. I wanted to deliver them myself. I decided to pick them up on the way home and take them and the phone to Kay. Surprise her by coming home early.

"Good idea," Ophie said with a smile that was too smug. She looked damn happy about something.

"I'm taking the rest of the day off, too."

Ophie nodded. "Of course, boss. It's your birthday. You deserve it. We can handle things here." She clutched my arm. "Happy birthday, Jus."

*Kayla*

I'd picked up the cake and set up for Justin's party. I wanted to wear something special tonight. I wanted to look glamorous for Jus before I became so big I waddled around, and serene and happy for our parents. We'd decided that it wouldn't be stealing Justin's birthday thunder to announce another birth at his party tonight. Why not when we had so many family and friends together?

I did my hair and makeup carefully. Put on my sexy new bra and panties—I'd already promised Jus another round of birthday sex after the party. And laid out three dresses I was trying to decide between on the bed.

I was about to try one on when the buzzer rang. Odd, why didn't whoever was there text? I expected it to be a delivery. I pulled on my robe and went to the entryway to answer it.

"Kayla? Lazer. Hope I'm not interrupting. I know you're busy getting ready for tonight. And I swear I'm not just an extremely early guest. But I have a present for Justin I wanted to drop off while I was in the area."

"I'll buzz you in." I pulled my silk robe tighter around me. There was no time to change before he got here.

A couple of minutes later, I was welcoming Lazer in.

He handed me a gift wrapped in birthday paper. "It's a peace offering for Justin." He looked a little shamefaced. "It needs an explanation. At first it seems self-serving. It's a collector's edition copy of the new video game."

"He'll love it!" I said. "Congrats on the release. The news is full of its success. One of the fastest-selling games in recent history."

Lazer nodded, looking almost modest. Complete modesty was asking too much of him. "Thanks in no small part to my awesome beta testers."

I stifled a laugh. Modesty didn't sit well on Lazer.

"It has a little special Easter egg in it for Justin and you. To be viewed in private." He wiggled his eyebrows suggestively.

I laughed.

He told me how to find it. "You'll want to play it together."

"You leave me curious. You won't tell me what it is?" I said.

"You'll find out soon enough." He shook his head. "It's my way of apologizing for hitting on his wife. I don't want things to be awkward between any of us." He took a deep breath. "And to come clean with you. When I first heard about Justin's surprise wedding, I suspected you of marrying him for his money."

"Didn't everyone? You were by no means alone, Sherlock."

He grinned. "I have a financial interest in Flash. Selfishly, I was afraid he'd made Flash vulnerable by marrying you."

"You thought I was going to divorce him and take half of his share?" I raised one eyebrow.

"Yeah. Do you blame me?"

I shrugged. "Does no one believe in love at, I'd guess you'd call it, second sight?"

"Money makes people more attractive."

"The curse of being a billionaire—is her love real? Or is her love for your money?"

"Damn, Kayla." He took a deep breath, looking apologetic again. "You're making this hard on me. I hit on you on purpose to see how you'd react. If you could be separated from him. If you'd just married him for his money.

"And then I surprised myself by feeling a spark between us. I thought you reciprocated. And...you know the rest. But something changed," he said. "You really love him."

"Don't sound so surprised! Of course I do." I shook my head. "Who wouldn't? Jus is sweet and adorable." I paused. "I'm sorry if I led you on."

"No, it's nothing." He paused again. "The path not taken. I just wanted to say this one time before we live the rest of our lives as good friends. I think you could have been the one. I think I would have fallen in love with you. Is that crazy?"

I had a lump in my throat. I opened my arms.

He pulled me into a tight, intimate hug.

"Not crazy at all. If not for Jus, I would have fallen in love with you. I'm sure of it." I smiled at him with tears in my eyes. This pregnancy was making me so emotional. "I'll always love you—"

*Justin*

I was on my way up the elevator in the penthouse with the balloons and flowers in my hand. Imagining the surprise on Kay's face when I came home early. Her cell phone buzzed in my pocket. I pulled it out out of habit. She had an email from Britt.

*Congrats, girl! Way to take advantage of the situation. You got pregnant ASAP!! Just like I told you to. Hook him for life. His money is yours. Did you flush the pills like I said? Ha ha! Whatever you do from now on doesn't matter. You're set for life! Money, money, money!!*

My stomach cramped up. I felt suddenly cold. No! No, Kay wouldn't...

But this was from her best friend. The woman she told everything to. The woman who helped her with the gift to tell me about the baby.

I took a deep breath as the elevator reached the penthouse. I had to get a grip. The elevator doors opened. Kay was in the entryway, wearing her thin, skimpy, sexy, short robe, wrapped intimately in Lazer's arms. Gazing into his eyes. And she was saying, "I'll always love you."

**Gina Robinson** is the award-winning author of the contemporary new adult romances *Rushed, Crushed, Reckless Longing, Reckless Secrets,* and *Reckless Together* and the Agent Ex series of humorous romantic suspense novels. She's currently working on the next installment of Switched at Marriage.

### Connect with Gina Online:

My Website: http://www.ginarobinson.com/
Twitter: @ginamrobinson
Facebook: www.facebook.com/GinaRobinsonAuthor